Liberty Letters

The personal correspondence of
Emma Edmonds *and* **Mollie Turner**

Civil War Spies, 1862

Nancy LeSourd

Zonder**kidz**

We want to hear from you. Please send your comments about this book to us in care of zreview@zondervan.com. Thank you.

Zonderkidz.

The children's group of Zondervan

www.zonderkidz.com

Liberty Letters: The Personal Correspondence of Emma Edmonds and Mollie Turner
Copyright © 2003 by Nancy Oliver LeSourd

This book is a work of fiction. References to real people, events, establishments, organizations, or locales are intended only to provide a sense of authenticity, and are used fictitiously. All other characters, and all incidents and dialogue, are drawn from the author's imagination and are not to be construed as real.

Requests for information should be addressed to:
Grand Rapids, Michigan 49530

ISBN: 0-310-70352-2

The story of Emma Edmonds as told in Emma's letters is adapted from Female Spy, 1864, republished as Nurse and Spy in the Union Army, 1865, by S. Emma E. Edmonds.

Winslow Homer, American, 1836-1910
Young Soldier: Separate Study of a Soldier Giving Water to a Wounded Companion, 1861 Oil, gouache, black crayon on canvas; 360 x 175 mm 14-7/8 x 6 7/8 in.); Cooper -Hewitt, National Design Museum, Smithsonian Institution Gift of Charles Savage Homer, Jr., 1912-12-110; Photo: Ken Pelka

Zonderkidz is a trademark of Zondervan.

Library of Congress Cataloging-in-Publication Data

LeSourd, Nancy.

The personal correspondence of Emma Edmonds and Mollie Turner : assignment--Civil War spies, 1862 / Nancy LeSourd.-- 1st ed.

p. cm. -- (Liberty letters)

Summary: Letters between two friends, one a nurse in Richmond, Virginia, and the other a soldier in Washington, D.C., chronicle their experiences during the Civil War, including their work as Union spies and their reliance on God.

ISBN 0-310-70352-2 (Hardcover)

[1. Spies--Fiction. 2. Nurses--Fiction. 3. Soldiers--Fiction. 4. Christian life--Fiction. 5. United States--History--Civil War, 1861-1865--Fiction. 6. Letters--Fiction.] I. Title.

PZ7.L56268Pf 2004

[Fic]--dc22

2003023558

Liberty Letters is a trademark of Nancy Oliver LeSourd.

Produced in association with the brand development agency of Evergreen Ideas, Inc., on behalf of Nancy LeSourd. For more information on Nancy LeSourd or the Liberty Letters series, visit www.Zonderkidz.com/libertyletters.

Editor: Gwen Ellis
Cover design: Michelle Lenger
Interior design: Tracey Moran
Photo layout design: Merit Alderink and Susan Ambs

Printed in the United States of America

04 05 06 07 /❖DC/ 10 9 8 7 6 5 4 3 2 1

For Cate and Luke

Richmond, Virginia

June 17, 1861

Dear Frank,

I couldn't believe my eyes. "Private Franklin Thompson, of the Second Michigan Volunteers," you said. "Requesting donations for the Union army, ma'am."

Great-Auntie Belle scurried around, loading my arms with linens, food, and medicines. So many questions swirled around in my head. How did you get to Michigan? And what, pray tell, possessed you to enlist in the Union army?

As you carried the supplies outside to the ambulance, you whispered, "You'll keep my secret, won't you, Mollie?"

"Such a nice young man, Mollie," Great-Auntie commented, arms filled with more donations.

"I think I know Private Thompson," I replied, "from last summer at church when I visited our cousins."

"Oh, how wonderful, dear! Why didn't you say something sooner?" She rushed outside and called you back in. "My great-niece thinks she knows you, young man. Were you in Connecticut last summer?"

"Why, yes I was," you replied coolly, "I sold Bibles before I enlisted. Are you Mollie? Mollie . . . Turner?" You made it seem like we were just casual friends when I know more about you than anyone else. I followed your lead, but Private Thompson, you have some explaining to do.

How clever of you to convince Great-Auntie that it would be so-o-o nice for a soldier far from home to receive the letters of a young girl—even a Confederate one. As you know from Great-Auntie's willingness to part with supplies for the Union, she makes no secret of her support for the Federal cause. Now that the Federal government has suspended mail service to the Southern states, Great-Auntie will make sure our letters get to and from Richmond through her private mail courier. Write to me soon. I will keep your secret, at least for now, but I want to know more.

Your friend,

Mollie

Washington, D.C.

June 22, 1861

Dear Mollie,

I know I need to explain. I was thankful for my job selling Bibles with Mr. Hurlburt's company in Connecticut. But, when he offered me the chance to work in Flint, Michigan, I jumped at the chance to see more of this adopted country of mine.

Letters of introduction from my church in Connecticut made it possible for me to stay in the home of a wonderful pastor and his family and I quickly made new friends. But, Mollie, although I always thought God called me from Canada to this country as a foreign missionary, never in a million years did I expect it might be to play a part in safeguarding these United States.

One day, this spring at the train station, I heard the newsboy cry out, "Fall of Fort Sumter—President's Proclamation—Call for 75,000 men!" It's true I'm not an American. I could return to my native land of Canada and escape all this turmoil. But when I heard the call from President Lincoln for men to fight for my adopted country, I couldn't turn away.

I wanted to express my gratitude to the people of the Northern states who not only adopted me as one of their own but also proclaimed loudly the need to free the slaves. After much prayer, I knew God meant for me to enlist in the army. So when my friends all volunteered for the Second Regiment of the Michigan Volunteer Infantry, I assumed God would make a way for me to join, too. But I missed the height requirement by two inches.

The day my friends left, the people of Flint gave them the grandest send-off. The boys lined up with their bright bayonets flashing in the morning sunlight. Almost every family had a father, husband, son, or brother in that band of soldiers. They told them good-bye, perhaps for years, perhaps forever. The pastor preached a sermon and presented a New Testament to each soldier. Then as the bands played the *Star-Spangled Banner*, the soldiers marched off to Washington. I wanted to be with them!

A few weeks later, who should return to Flint but my old friend from church, William Morse, now *Captain* William Morse, who had come back to recruit more soldiers for Company F of the Second Michigan Regiment.

This time I was ready. I stuffed my shoes with paper and stood as tall as I could. It worked! What a glorious day! I was now Private Franklin Thompson of Company F of the Second Michigan Volunteer Infantry of the United States Army.

When I got to Washington, the army assigned me to be a field nurse. I reported to the surgeon-in-charge and received my first order to visit the temporary hospitals set up all over the city. Although there are no battle injuries yet, many are sick with typhoid and malaria. There are not enough beds for the sick; not enough doctors to treat them; and not enough medicines and food.

That's why some of us decided to visit the good ladies of Washington and plead with them to donate to the Union. That was the day I saw you again—a most fortunate day for me. I hope you feel the same.

Your friend,

Frank

Company F, Second Michigan Regiment

Richmond, Virginia

June 25, 1861

Dear Frank,

I still can't believe it was you. There in my great-auntie's parlor. There, dressed in the blue uniform of the Federals. How do you think you can pull this off—being a private in the United States Army? Sure you can handle nursing duties. But what about shooting and riding a horse, marching and drilling, standing guard and picket duty? Can you keep your secret for much longer? I think not.

Do not think that just because my great-aunt is pro-Union that I necessarily follow in her footsteps—although I am sure both she and Great-Uncle Chester would be delighted if I did. The Greats (that's what I call them) moved from Boston to Washington ten years ago so Great-Uncle Chester could teach at the hospital and open his surgery practice. To the great embarrassment of my Richmond kin, Great-Uncle Chester is now a surgeon with the Union army and Great-Auntie Belle is an outspoken supporter of President Lincoln and his policies.

For years before this war began, Momma rolled her eyes and shook her head every time Daddy announced that the Greats were coming to visit. Momma was sure they came just to create mischief with their pro-abolition talk. I, on the other hand, would beg Daddy to let me go with him to collect them from the train station. I could not get enough time with them, for no matter how young I was, they acted as if what I had to say had importance. Great-Auntie Belle would ask my opinion and nod thoughtfully at what I had to say. Great-Uncle Chester would stroke his beard and then tap Great-Auntie on the arm, and say, "The young'un has a point, my dear." I often heard him say proudly to Daddy, "That gal of yours has a good head on those pretty shoulders."

Daddy's Northern upbringing marked him as well. But, in deference to Momma and her kin, Daddy kept his opinions to himself. A few years ago, before Daddy got sick and died, I overheard Daddy tell Momma that there was growing talk of secession from the Union. One day, the Southern states might set up their own government.

Momma told Daddy that if such attitudes continued, brother might be forced to fight against brother. When Daddy agreed, Momma cried on his shoulder for nearly an hour and twisted her handkerchief into a soggy knot. After that, Daddy never said another word about these possibilities—at least not out loud. He loved Momma too much to upset her.

But oh, how he loved it when the Greats came to visit. I saw the sparkle in his eyes when the Greats argued with Daddy's business acquaintances and friends about the preservation of the Union at all costs. He enjoyed every moment.

Your friend,

Mollie

Richmond, Virginia

June 28, 1861

Dear Frank,

Today Momma and I went to Mrs.Whitfield's home to sew uniforms for the soldiers. We'd barely walked in the door when we heard the ladies' angry voices. Mrs. Whitfield whispered she had personally delivered a handwritten invitation to Miss Elizabeth Van Lew and her mother to join them to sew for the Confederate soldiers, but the Van Lews refused to come.

"Let's not forget they sent their daughter, Betty, to that Quaker school in Philadelphia," an outraged Mrs. Morris reminded everyone. "They filled that child's head with abolition talk and it changed her forever."

"That they did," Mrs. Forrest agreed, "and, when Mr. Van Lew died, Betty talked her mother into freeing all their slaves."

Aunt Lydia added, "I heard they even sent one of their slave girls up north to Philadelphia for her schooling and paid for it all!"

I watched the ladies ram their needles through the flannel shirts they were stitching with as much force as the words they were speaking. I kept my head lowered and like Daddy, I kept my opinions to myself. This talk was far different from times before Virginia left the Union. These same ladies enjoyed receiving invitations to the Van Lew mansion on Church Hill to meet famous men and women.

Personally, I think these ladies are petty gossips. Everyone has a right to his own opinion, doesn't he? Or perhaps not. Perhaps, in war, one must always choose sides. I am still not sure what I think. If I had to choose, I'm not sure which side I would support. The Greats are committed to the Union, Momma and her kin to the Confederacy. I wish Daddy were here to help me talk this through.

I suspect before this war is over, I will indeed be forced to choose a side. But until then, I shall stay happily in the middle. I still knit for the Confederates, but this pair of socks is included for you, my adventurous Union friend. Perhaps they will keep your feet from blistering on those long marches.

Your friend,

Mollie

Richmond, Virginia

June 29, 1861

Dear Frank,

Great-Auntie writes that Washington is no longer the same with so many soldiers encamped around it. She tells time now by the sound of bugles and drums, instead of the clocks. The girls in Richmond are excited about this war and push their brothers, cousins, and boyfriends to enlist in the Confederate army. Thousands go out of the city each afternoon to watch the evening drills.

Sissy is the worst of all. She may be two years older than I, but she has such romantic notions about this war. But then, so do most of our friends. Sissy thinks she can just send Lemuel off to war and he will return to her a hero.

Some of our friends argue over which units have the most adorable boys in them! They ride out by horseback and carriage each afternoon to bat their eyelashes at the boys in gray coats and butternut-colored pants. Of course, the soldiers seem to think this war is an excuse for a party, too. After the drills and pageantry, they socialize with all the beautiful girls who come to see them each day.

The adults gather at the Spotswood Hotel where President and Mrs. Davis are staying while their mansion is being prepared for them. The people beg President Davis for a speech. He gives one sometimes right in front of the hotel. Nearly every day he mounts his horse and rides out to the camps to inspect the troops. New regiments of soldiers arrive by train and march down the Richmond streets singing "Dixie," while girls wave handkerchiefs at them. Ladies gather to gossip and sew Confederate flags and uniforms.

It's all one great party here. Everyone thinks we will simply wallop the North in one big battle, and then it will all be over. I am not so sure. And what is to come of this? Broken hearts. Broken bodies. A broken nation.

Your friend,

Mollie

Washington, D.C.

June 30, 1861

Dear Mollie,

Your letter of a few days ago arrived. As for riding a horse or shooting a gun, what do you think I did all those years when I was growing up on our farm in New Brunswick, Canada? I can outride and outshoot most anyone—thank you, Miss Mollie. If God has called me to this, then he has prepared me and equipped me to do what I must do. If I am found out, it will not be because I failed to hold my own with these brave men.

And don't think nursing duty isn't hard work. Each camp sets up a temporary hospital to take care of about twenty-five men. The field nurses ready the buildings by leveling the ground, laying boards for the floor, and setting up the tents. Even when they are off duty, they dig drains around the tents, plant evergreens and put up awnings to help provide shade for the patients from this horrible heat.

I'm sorry if I seem to be short with you. I'm very tired. The makeshift hospitals in churches and schools overflow with sick soldiers. The surgeons make the rounds visiting them twice a day if they can, and I nurse these soldiers in several hospitals round the clock.

Your friend,

Frank

Richmond, Virginia

July 2, 1861

Dear Frank,

Yesterday Sissy married Lemuel Hastings. And today he enlisted in the Army of the Confederate States of America. Sissy is determined to follow him wherever he is sent to fight. Momma is horrified. She told Sissy today that her place is in Richmond with the ladies, sewing uniforms, knitting socks, and rolling bandages. Sissy bounced out of the room with her skirts swishing behind her as she tossed her head full of blonde curls. "I shall follow Lemuel to the ends of the earth," she called back to us over her shoulder. "It is my wifely duty."

Sissy has always been impulsive, but she gave Momma only four days to pull together a wedding. Even with the help of Momma's kin, and their servants, there was hardly enough time to decorate the parlor, bake and display the cakes and sweets, and deliver all the invitations. Sissy decided there should be no wedding gifts. Not that anyone has any money to spare right now, anyway. In her usual fashion, she turned that all to her advantage. In her noblest of voices, she announced to one and all that they should each bring a necessity for the Confederate soldiers and deposit it in the box by the front door.

I honestly don't believe that Sissy understands what this is all about. She probably thinks she will pull on her white kidskin gloves, button up her dainty shoes, and swirl her hooped skirt around her as she travels by train or coach to the nearest town where Lemuel's unit is stationed. Then when he is off duty, they will dance the night away at the local town hall.

Your friend,

Mollie

Richmond, Virginia

July 3, 1861

Dear Frank,

I can't return to Mrs. Pegram's school next fall. The Greats paid for my education for the past two years since Daddy died but now Mrs. Pegram has returned their greenbacks. Mrs. Pegram told them that Federal dollars are worthless to purchase an education for a Confederate girl. She said they could exchange their money for Confederate scrip and resend the funds for my semester's tuition.

Of course, that made the Greats furious. As much as they value my education, they won't put it ahead of their beliefs. The next week, Great-Auntie prepared a box of books from Great-Uncle Chester's library and sent them to me to study on my own.

I can understand the Pegrams' point of view. While Mrs. Pegram teaches the girls on Franklin Street, her three sons fight for the Confederacy. That's my problem. I can see and understand both sides of this war. I wish I had the passion of the Greats, or the Pegrams, or you. I just don't know what I believe.

My good friend, Charlie, brought the newspapers today. We spread them out on the table on the veranda. The Confederates captured the Union steamer, the *St. Nicolas*. The paper reported that Madame LaForce—an outrageously dressed, veiled lady—boarded at Baltimore with great fanfare and seven dress trunks. Madame LaForce flirted with the sailors in French and English and later retired to check on her trunks filled not with dresses but with pistols and swords. It turns out Madame LaForce was really Colonel Thomas! "She" created such a distraction that no one noticed the eight men who boarded the *St. Nicolas* at Port Comfort that day and then joined Colonel Thomas in the attack on the ship that night. Later, the *St. Nicolas* captured several other Union ships filled with coffee and ice and other supplies that can now go to the Confederate army.

Ooh la la!! Perhaps my French lessons at Mrs. Pegram's School will not go to waste. I can disguise myself as a French mademoiselle and take over a ship!

Your friend,

Mollie

Richmond, Virginia

July 4, 1861

Dear Frank,

It was a grand day for celebrating our nation's independence, but I had to wonder—were the Richmond folk celebrating our independence from England years ago or from the Union now?

The day began with an eleven-gun salute to the eleven Confederate states and continued with parades, and speeches, and picnics. As usual, my friends rode out to the camps outside the city to watch the men march and drill and parade and show off. The girls swooned with delight as the soldiers marched past. They brought baskets of food to share with their favorite regiments after the drills.

Some say the Alabama troops are the most handsome. Others say the Carolina troops are the most well mannered. Still others like the rugged looks and horsemanship of the Texans. I think it is all so silly. Will these girls talk this way if these boys come back maimed and disfigured from the battlefield?

Your friend,

Mollie

Washington, D.C.

July 5, 1861

Dear Mollie,

Washington is overrun with soldiers. White tents dot the landscape all around the city. The Capitol and the White House shelter hundreds of soldiers, who sit around playing cards, and wait for action. Thousands of soldiers drill in the streets. Blasts from bugles and the rat-a-tat of drums fill the air.

All are eager to fight. The rebellion should be put down quickly. Thank you for keeping my secret this long—and if you will, longer still.

Your friend,

Frank

Richmond, Virginia

July 9, 1861

Dear Frank,

Received your good letter, Frank, but do not suppose this to be a short war. You think the boys in blue will crush the boys in gray. But here in Richmond, we too have white tents dotting the landscape like snow. We too have soldiers marching day and night, eager to meet the enemy. We too have hundreds, if not thousands, of young men who are certain we will capture Washington and take over the White House and Capitol where your soldiers now lounge.

I do not think victory will come so easily, my dear friend, not to either side.

Your troubled friend,

Mollie

Richmond, Virginia

July 10, 1861

Dear Frank,

Sissy and I walked to Pizzini's for ice cream. With each bite, Sissy complained about the Union blockade of our ports. If it succeeds, we will be unable to get the necessities of life. To Sissy, this means her tea and sweets. She hoards sugar in a tin can in her room. She says she may have to suffer many things in this war, but she will not suffer the loss of her sugar.

Sissy wants this silly war to get started so those horrible Yanks can be put in their place and her dear Lem can come home to her. I suppose that is what you are to most of those I know here: a horrible Yank.

Day after day, we knit socks and scarves for the Confederates. It is hard to handle the wool on these hot summer days. Yet, Momma is right, the soldiers will be glad of the warmth of these socks and scarves come winter. Because I am still not sure what I think of this war effort, I pretend these socks will go only to Lemuel. It is all right, of course, to knit socks for one's family no matter what one might think about the war.

Your friend,

Mollie

Richmond, Virginia

July 13, 1861

Dear Frank,

The Northern papers Great-Auntie sent me cheer you Federals on to stop the "Rebel Congress" from meeting next week. "Forward to Richmond! On to Richmond! 'The Rebel Congress' shall not meet." I admit I am frightened. Momma, too. She speaks in hushed tones with the Richmond kin. They are especially quiet around Sissy. I don't think they want her to be frightened for Lemuel. But how can she not be frightened? Won't he be one of the ones defending our dear city?

Will you be the one attacking it? I do not like this at all.

This afternoon, Lemuel came by the house to tell Sissy that his regiment leaves in the next few days. His voice sounded strong and sure as he tried to reassure her. "Don't worry, I'll be back very soon."

Sissy twisted her curls as she studied Lemuel, who stood tall and handsome in his gray jacket and butternut pants with his sword nearly touching the floor. Suddenly, she threw herself in his arms and sobbed, "Oh, Lem. I can't let you go!"

Lemuel held her close and echoed what we all hoped that day. "Dearest wife, do not despair. This will be a short war without much fighting. Peace is what both the North and the South want."

Momma and I gave Lem a big hug and then left Sissy and Lem alone to say their good-byes.

Are you marching now, too? Yes, I shall continue to keep your secret. Do not fear. You must do what you must. Perhaps I am envious of you, because I don't have a committed zeal toward either side of this war. I admire the fact that you know what you believe, and you are willing to fight for it. How can I deny you that right? You must know, dear Frank, that just as you trusted me with your secret in Connecticut, so now can you trust me with your secret in Virginia. I shall be a true friend to you, as I know you will be to me.

Please be careful.

Your friend,

Mollie

Richmond, Virginia

July 17, 1861

Dear Frank,

Just three days until the Confederate government meets here in Richmond. The delegates have arrived by railroad and coach from all over the South. Most have taken rooms at the Spotswood Hotel. They move about the city with an air of importance. Yet they are strangers to us.

For weeks now, these new officials have had something to say as day after day companies march out. So far, it has been a war of words—words that will not be enough to protect us if the Federals are on the way here to stop the Confederate Congress from meeting.

But today a hush of fear hangs over this city. The quiet does not still the steady drone of heavy artillery and the muffled beats of the distant drummers. Sissy sits at the window, twisting her handkerchief first one way then the other. Momma told her to knit to keep her fingers busy. Sissy tried, but gave up in frustration, dropping more stitches than she could keep on the needles.

I suggested a walk. We found the streets of Richmond quiet. Old men spoke in hushed tones in doorways. Women whispered to one another behind fans. Only the youngest children seemed carefree. Would the Union win and be "On to Richmond?" What about the dozens of fathers, husbands, brothers, and sons that enlisted? Would they return?

Tonight Momma and the Richmond ladies gathered at Aunt Lydia's home to roll bandages and pick lint for packing wounds. Momma asked Sissy and me to come with her. I wish we were knitting socks and sewing uniform shirts. I don't like preparing for wounds and cuts and bloody bodies. I shudder to think of it. Sissy tries to join in, but I can see on her face she is wondering if the bandage she rolls tonight will be on her husband tomorrow.

The wait is awful. If only we had news.

Your friend,

Mollie

Richmond Virginia

July 19, 1861

Dear Frank,

We awoke to the news that General Beauregard won the first fight with the Union in Manassas. The city today bustled with excitement and anxiety—excitement because the Confederates scored a victory and anxiety because we wondered at what cost.

Surgeons in ambulances, our bandages with them, raced to Manassas. Sissy was desperate to go with them, but Momma would not permit it. Word came that more fighting is expected and that the skirmish yesterday was just a prelude. Sissy has given up twisting her handkerchief and twists her hair now. "I just have to know if Lem is all right," she said to me more than once today.

I have to know if you are all right. Were you there? Did you fight today? Are you well?

I caught Sissy packing tonight. I told Momma because I knew Sissy would do something crazy—like leave in the middle of the night—just to make sure Lemuel is safe. But *she* would not be safe. Sissy was angry with me, but I don't care. I love my sister.

Your friend,

Mollie

Richmond, Virginia

July 21, 1861

Dear Frank,

    President Davis left on the train to Manassas this morning. I tried to get back into Sissy's good graces by walking with her from St. Paul's to the Spotswood Hotel for news. The First Lady moved quietly about the lobby, speaking first to one and then to another mother, wife, or daughter of our men and boys in gray who were fighting that day. We overheard someone tell her that the fighting has been going on since six o'clock this morning at Manassas. Sissy swallowed hard and clenched her hands. I gave her my handkerchief so she would have something to twist.

    It was all I could do to get Sissy to leave the Spotswood Hotel tonight to return home. She was sure news would come swiftly to the hotel because the wives of so many colonels and generals as well as the First Lady of the Confederacy were there. True enough. I could see in their eyes that they would stay up all night until they had news.

    It is the waiting, the uncertainty, that is so difficult to bear.

Your friend,

Mollie

Richmond, Virginia

July 22, 1861

Dear Frank,

This Monday morning we were up before dawn. I don't think Sissy, Momma, or I slept much last night. Word of the battle and victory for the South spread quickly. Richmond should have been excited, but most of the women just wanted to know one thing—the fate of their loved ones.

I spent most of my day with Sissy at the Virginia Central train station hoping for word of Lemuel. We waited for the train from Manassas in the pouring rain until after ten at night. When it was clear we would hear no word of Lemuel tonight, we went home, tired and soaked to the skin. Sissy fell asleep exhausted as soon as I helped her out of her wet clothes.

Tomorrow, we should know about Lem. But what about you? I pray you are safe.

Your friend,

Mollie

Richmond, Virginia

July 23, 1861

Dear Frank,

Early this morning we went back down to the train depot. President Davis arrived from Manassas on the first train. He said the Confederates sent the Yankees running toward Washington. The papers all declared victory, but we cannot celebrate until we know if Lemuel is safe. Dozens of soldiers, bloody and wounded, poured out of the train cars. Sissy stood on a box and looked at each face for her Lem.

Men and boys with wounded arms and legs on stretchers. Bloody bandages on the heads and arms of those who could walk. Men and boys limping and on crutches. Where were our lively marchers now? No drums or bugles welcomed these soldiers. Only women and girls, anxious to see someone they dearly love.

This afternoon, the train brought another load of desperate soldiers from Manassas. We saw Elijah Wilson, our good friend who had enlisted with Lem. Sissy raced to Elijah whose head was bloody and bandaged. "Elijah, are you all right? You're bleeding! You must come home with us tonight."

Elijah's wound is not too deep, and he should be fine. He enjoyed the good food Momma prepared, and we got much news from him about the battle. Elijah did not know Lem's present whereabouts, but he had seen him toward the end of the battle. At that time, he had still been standing strong. That news comforted Sissy and she brightened enough to share her sugar with Elijah in the tea Momma made for him. When he spoke of the falling Federals, though, I could not help but think of you. I hope you were not one of those in blue who fell on Sunday, the Sabbath day of our Lord.

Tonight, my good friend, Charlie, brought by a copy of the *Examiner.* The paper said, "By the work of Sunday we have broken the backbone of the invasion and utterly broken the spirit of the North." Perhaps so. But trains continue to bring in the dead and the wounded, and homes have turned into hospitals.

Charlie told us that hundreds of Union prisoners were arriving at the train station and being marched through the streets to Liggon's tobacco factory on Main Street. If there are Federals here now in our city, then there must be Confederates captured as well. This has Sissy severely agitated as she wonders if Lem is captured. She twists both hair and handkerchief. Momma had her knead some bread tonight just to keep her hands busy as well as her mind.

Your worried friend,
but one who is not yet given over to twisting,

Mollie

Richmond, Virginia

July 26, 1861

Dear Frank,

Oh glory hallelujah! After days of waiting and searching among the wounded, Sissy finally heard from Lem. He is safe, still with both arms and both legs. Determined more than ever to follow him, Sissy packed her bags and wouldn't listen at all to Momma who begged her to stay. Momma and I took Sissy to the train depot this morning, and now it is Momma who twists her handkerchief. I kissed Sissy good-bye and told her I would go with her the next time. That only agitated Momma more. Sissy talked a blue streak because she is so excited about seeing Lem again. Lem was promoted to captain for his bravery in action at the Battle of Manassas, and Sissy stayed up all night to stitch him a new shirt to show him how proud she is of him. I must admit; it is a huge improvement over her first effort—the shirt with two right sleeves.

After we saw Sissy off, Momma and I went to Aunt Lydia's to pick some more lint and roll some more bandages. But mostly, it was to get the news. And we were not disappointed! Much has been going on in the last few days.

Did you know the Yankee women traveled from Washington to the battle in their buggies and coaches with their picnic hampers, brandy and fruit? Well, they got the surprise of their lives when they had to step over dead soldiers to scurry back to the safety of their Washington homes. The Richmond ladies told Momma they always knew Northern women lacked compassion. Not at all like our own Sally Tompkins, they murmured.

Judge Robertson moved his family to the country and turned over his house at Main and Third streets to Miss Sally Tompkins to use as a hospital. She stocked it with extra beds, clean linens, medicines, and nourishing foods. The ladies approve of her decision to use her family fortune to relieve our men's suffering. They all plan to help Miss Sally in any way they can.

As quick as they were to praise Sally Tompkins, they tripped over each other to condemn another Richmond lady, Miss Betty Van Lew. "Always peculiar in her thinking," they said. "A Northerner through and through," they agreed. "Dangerous to the Confederacy," they feared.

Mrs. Adams exclaimed, "I heard the Yankees had not even had time to peruse their new surroundings before Miss Van Lew was at the prison door begging to nurse them." Mrs. Whitfield added, "Of course that young prison warden, Lieutenant Todd, put her in her place and told her under no uncertain terms would a Southern lady do such a thing."

"But you know what she did then?" exclaimed Mrs. Adams. "She went from office to office until she could convince someone to let her visit the Federal prisoners!"

Mrs. Martin added, "I heard she brings them sweets and books and stationery."

Mrs. Logan put down her lint basket and leaned across the table. She spoke in a very quiet voice, "You know, dear ladies, that it is not so much what she brings in that concerns me." They all leaned forward eagerly. "It's what she brings out!"

All the Richmond ladies picking lint and rolling bandages nodded knowingly. What were they talking about? Do they think Miss Van Lew is a spy? Why they hang spies! Surely she doesn't believe so much in the Union cause that she would put her life on the line like that?

It was a most troubling conversation. I ask myself if there is anything I believe in so strongly that I would risk danger to myself to further its cause? If I were a sixteen-year-old boy, instead of a sixteen-year-old girl, would I run off to join the army or would I use the excuse that I am too young to enlist?

Several months ago, when the states began seceding from the Union, the newspapers warned that there might be Federal loyalists among us. They said that Richmond contained a large number of secret enemies of the South, "in petticoats as well as pantaloons." I think the petticoats they were referring to belong to Miss Van Lew. But are there others? Are women and girls spying for the Union? Do they spy for the Confederacy, too?

Your friend,

Mollie

Richmond, Virginia

July 28, 1861

Dear Frank,

President Davis requested that we honor today, Sunday, as a day of thanksgiving for the Confederate victory. While the preacher spoke about the hand of God being with the South, I had to wonder if the hand of God was with the North as well.

I know of your good heart, and your strong relationship with Jesus. I know that wherever you go, you speak of him to others. Selling Bibles was just another way for you to help people learn about him. So, was God with you in this battle? Are you having a day of thanksgiving? Is God with you only when you win a battle—or is he there when you lose?

Momma misses Sissy. She thinks Sissy is too young to be traveling alone especially in this wartime, but Sissy is a married woman now and eighteen. She'll be fine. Momma busied herself on the Sabbath making a pie, using some of Sissy's precious hoarded sugar. Momma would never have done that if she were not so worried.

Charlie brought by the *Examiner.* He knows I love to read what the papers are saying. He stayed to talk a bit. Charlie is itching to go to war, but at fourteen, his parents have forbidden him to try to enlist until he turns sixteen. He counts down the days. They say a boy must be at least eighteen before he can enlist, but I know boys sixteen and seventeen who wear the gray jackets of the Confederacy. I suppose if they fooled the recruiters, you could, too. Charlie practices drumming the signals so that perhaps he can join his brother's unit as a drummer boy before much longer. Until then, he pours over the papers to learn as much as he can.

Charlie and I drank lemonade on the veranda with one of Momma's last lemons (without Sissy's sugar) and read the paper. I could not believe their vicious attack on Miss Van Lew and her mother. First it praised all the true women of Richmond who have been giving their aid to the wounded. But then it told of the kindnesses Miss Betty and her mother have shown toward the Yankee prisoners just four blocks from their home. The *Examiner* said that "the course of these two females in providing them with delicacies, buying them books, stationery and papers, cannot but be regarded as an evidence of sympathy amounting to an endorsement of the cause and conduct of these Northern vandals."

Wait until the Richmond ladies read this! Miss Van Lew will never be invited to sew with these ladies again. Somehow, I don't think she will mind at all.

Your friend,

Mollie

Richmond, Virginia

August 2, 1861

Dear Frank,

Sissy is back! It was a short visit, but she is gloriously happy. She had gotten herself worked up thinking that maybe Lem was really all cut up, bloodied, or even missing an arm or leg and didn't want to frighten her. Sissy worked that scenario over and over in her mind until it became real. Until she saw Lem with her own eyes, she was not going to be satisfied.

Momma is very happy to have her back home. Sissy stitched all the way back on the train. Even Momma has to admit her handiwork is getting much better. Sissy says every stitch is filled with love for her Lem.

I took Sissy with me to Pizzini's this afternoon to meet our friends. The price of a dish of ice cream is double what it was earlier this summer, so Sissy and I shared a bowl. All our friends wanted to know about Lem and Sissy's exciting trip to see him. Sissy, of course, exaggerated to create a better story. The girls enjoyed it greatly.

Emily arrived with a new friend, Louly Wigfall. Her father used to be the senator from Texas when we were an undivided nation. Now he commands the First Texas Regiment that drills at a camp outside our city. Louly asked about Mrs. Pegram's School and my friends gladly filled her in on what a great school it is. Sissy suggested we walk over to see the new president's mansion which all the girls wanted to do and there was no more talk about Mrs. Pegram's School. I squeezed Sissy's hand under the table to thank her. I do miss my schooling. I read the books Great-Auntie sends me, but it is not the same.

Your friend,

Mollie

Washington, D.C.

August 10, 1861

Dear Mollie,

Your letters finally caught up with me, and I have read each of them several times. I have had very little time to write, but now I will try to tell you all that has happened these last three weeks.

When we began our march to Manassas, the bands played patriotic songs, and the soldiers cried out enthusiastically, "On to Richmond!" But I felt strangely out of harmony with the wild, joyous spirit of the troops. As I rode slowly along in the ambulance, watching those long lines of bayonets gleaming and flashing in the sunlight, I thought that many—very many—of these men might never return. Even if the victory was to be ours, and I had no doubt it would be, many noble lives might be sacrificed to obtain it.

The first night of the march, we stayed in Fairfax. The men, exhausted from the long march in the July heat, slept well that evening. Early the next morning, the drummers and buglers sounded reveille, and the whole camp was up and marching again.

The heat continued, and there was little water. We did not even cross a stream where we could fill our canteens. About noon, we heard sharp volleys of muskets, but it turned out to be our advance guard firing at anything that moved. Every hour, we expected to meet the enemy.

The army moved steadily on and investigated every field, building, and ravine for miles in front and to the right and to the left. When we reached Centerville, we stopped for the night. Tired from two days of marching, the men fell in a heap. Many of their feet were blistered raw. We took linen, bandages, lint, and ointment and ministered to their blistered trodden feet.

The surgeons ordered the field nurses to prepare for the coming battle by securing several buildings, including a stone church, as makeshift hospitals and operating theaters. I helped set up medicine bottles, bandages, and the surgeon's tools.

Our chaplain and his wife are good friends of mine and a great comfort to our men. Chaplain B. always seems to know just what to say, and Mrs. B. is a great help to the field nurses. I know women can't serve as nurses on the battle-field, but Mrs. B. gives comfort to our boys by bringing them water and tending to them in the hospitals.

Late in the evening, Chaplain and Mrs. B. and I walked through the entire camp to see how the boys were doing, on this, the eve of their first battle. Some were writing letters home and enclosing keepsakes like locks of hair or rings, just in case. Others were reading their Bibles. Others sat in groups, talking in low tones. Many were stretched out on the ground, wrapped up in their blankets, oblivious to the dangers of the coming day.

We were about to return to our quarters when we heard singing coming from a little grove of trees not far from camp. When we came closer, we could hear the words of the hymn sung with great feeling:

O, for a faith that will not shrink, though pressed by every foe;
That will not tremble on the brink of any earthly woe.
That will not murmur or complain beneath the chastening rod
But in the hour of grief and pain will lean upon its God.

Chaplain B. said he recognized Willie Lyman's voice. Willie prayed for loved ones at home, for his comrades, for victory in battle. And with great emotion, he pled with God to comfort and support his mother if he should die. Others joined him in prayer, and then one by one, they shared with the others their faith in the power of the gospel of Christ.

We retired for the night greatly encouraged. But I could not help wondering if the Confederates on the other side of Bull Run were also grouped together praying for victory. *Oh, Lord, help us all*, I prayed, before I too, exhausted from the march and the preparation for tomorrow's battle, fell asleep.

I will write more soon, but am called to the bedside of a dying soldier. Until then, I am

Your faithful friend,

Frank

Washington, D.C.

August 11, 1861

Dear Mollie,

Despite the best care of our surgeon and our nurses, dear Willie Lyman, the boy I wrote to you about last night, died early this morning. His wounds from the battle were too grave for him to recover. After Chaplain B. prayed with him, Willie asked me to write to his mother. I took down every word he said, but it was all I could do to keep the tears from flowing on the paper and smearing the ink. His last words were, "Tell Mother I died trusting in Jesus." I cut a lock of his hair to put in the envelope with the letter. Oh, if only his dear mother could have been here to hold his hand. His soul winged its way to heaven as the first rays of the early morning light shown down.

I could not help but think about the contrast of the activities on these battlefields on this Sabbath day with what was happening in churches all over the states—Northern and Southern. While church members fall to their knees in prayer and church bells ring out the call to worship, their brothers, fathers, and sons fall to their knees struck with bullets as bugles and drums beat out the call to arms.

The Sunday of the battle began very early with column after column of soldiers marching over green hills and through the hazy valley in the remains of the moonlight. We heard no drums or bugles—only muffled marching of soldiers and the rumble of cannons. The three divisions each took a position along Bull Run Creek. As morning light broke, the two armies were in plain sight of each other. I delivered my horse to Jack, our hospital man, with strict orders to remain where he was, sensing that I might need my horse at any moment.

Chaplain B., Mrs. B., and I stood there, waiting for the first casualty. Mrs. B. is so brave. The field nurses, as you know, are all enlisted men, but no one was going to turn her away on a day like this. Mrs. B's narrow-brimmed leghorn hat sat firmly on her dark brown hair and framed her pale face and blue eyes. She had her silver-mounted, seven-shooter pistol tucked in her belt, a canteen of water swung over one shoulder, a flask of brandy over the other shoulder, and a haversack with lint, ointment, adhesive plaster, and bandages hanging by her side.

As the battle commenced, I raced to one of our wounded, and when I raised his head, now covered in blood, I saw it was Willie Lyman. Another nurse and I carried him on a stretcher to the ambulance. I spent most of the early morning and on into the day going from one fallen soldier to another.

The surgeon sent me back to Centerville for a fresh supply of lint and bandages. The distance was seven miles, and I went on horseback as fast as I could. When I returned, the field was covered with our wounded, dead, and dying.

Worried, I looked around for Mrs. B. For a few moments, I became sick with fear when I could not see her. Then I saw her upon her horse galloping toward me with all possible speed. About fifty canteens hung from the pommel of her saddle. "The troops are famished for water!" she exclaimed.

I mounted my horse, and we raced to the nearest spring where we filled the canteens as quickly as we could. Minnie balls fell thick and fast around us but we dodged those bullets and it was worth it to see the looks of appreciation on our men's faces as they took long drinks of the water. Chaplain B's horse was shot dead right out from under him. We went back and forth to the spring for three hours, filling canteens and distributing the water among the wounded. Then the Confederates pushed us back and captured the spring. Our source of water was gone.

Mrs. B. and I dismounted and went to work among the wounded alongside the surgeons and other nurses. Colonel Cameron rode up and dashed along the line shouting, "Come on, boys, the Rebels are in full retreat." But they were not. In fact, fresh supports had arrived to help them. The enemy advanced, and the panic-stricken crowds who had come to watch the fighting now joined the Federal troops retreating toward Washington.

I returned to the stone church in Centerville as fast as my horse would take me and began my work among the wounded. Many would not survive the horrible surgeries where shattered arms and legs are amputated. One boy asked me if I thought he would die before the morning. I asked him, "Does death hold any terrors for you?" He replied, "Oh no, I shall soon be asleep in Jesus."

We were so busy taking care of wounded or dying soldiers that we did not notice the Federal troops had pulled back and left us in Rebel-controlled territory. Surely they wouldn't leave the hospital of their own wounded in the clutches of the enemy! I had to find out for myself.

I walked back to the heights where I had seen the troops stack their guns, but no troops were there. I thought they must have changed position, but I could not find them anywhere. I had just started back to Centerville to the field hospital when suddenly I heard the Rebel cavalry. I hid in the brush until they passed and then made my way by cover of darkness back to Centerville.

By the time I got there, Chaplain and Mrs. B. had left for Washington. They took my horse with them because they thought I had been taken prisoner. I, too, needed to escape before the Rebels gained control over Centerville. But how could I leave those hospitals full of dying men without anyone to give them so much as a drink of water? Even at the risk of being captured, I had to go back to the stone church.

I gave water to as many as I could from my canteen. They begged me to leave before the Rebels arrived. I protested for a long time, but they insisted that I go. They said the Rebels would not let me tend their wounds or give them water to drink. They said the surgeons needed me. I left water as near their reach as possible and took my leave.

That night was exceedingly dark and the rain came down in torrents. I climbed a fence, crossed some lots, and made my way to Washington as quickly as possible. I had neither food nor water, but I kept safe the special items those wounded soldiers had entrusted into my care—letters, rings, pictures of loved ones, and messages that I would later send to their families.

Chaplain and Mrs. B. were thrilled to see me. I was thrilled to see my horse had not fallen into enemy hands, but would be there to ride with me another day.

It was a terrible, terrible battle for the Federals. If the Rebels had only kept coming, they might have captured Washington. I don't know why they didn't, but I am glad.

Your friend,

Frank

Richmond, Virginia

August 24, 1861

Dear Frank,

Today Momma and I volunteered our services to Miss Sally Tompkins, who runs Robertson Hospital. She is well suited for the task. There are twenty-two beds in the hospital, and although Miss Sally is not in the army, it is clear who the general is here!

I think even the Greats would be impressed with Miss Sally—despite her strong Confederate leanings. Especially Great-Uncle Chester. As you know, he loves it when Southern women display a "good head on their shoulders" and take matters into their own hands. I have heard him say more than once that Southern women are the ones who need to rebel!

The Robertson Hospital is spotless. There are clean linens every day and careful attention to hygiene. I think Miss Sally takes the motto "Cleanliness is next to godliness" quite seriously. She insists that the floors, bed linens, clothes, and the surgeon's tools are scrubbed clean. Her house servants are there to help her, but she is a bundle of energy herself. She carries her medicine kit on her belt at all times and ministers to the needs of these fallen soldiers.

As much as she cares for the body, she cares for the soul as well. She holds a prayer meeting every night and a Bible study as well. Momma and I stayed for tonight's meeting, and it brought tears to my eyes. Miss Sally loves the Lord very much, and her care for these soldiers comes from the depth of her love for the Lord. If a soldier is too ill or wounded to make it to the room for Bible study and prayer, she goes to his bedside to pray with him.

I like Miss Sally. I want to come here as often as possible to help her nurse the soldiers. See, I can do what you do, Pvt. Franklin Thompson, but I do not have to put myself in harm's way to do it. I still do not understand why you enlisted in the army at such great risk to yourself and your secret. I have a pass to visit Great-Auntie next month so we can finally talk about your secret.

Speaking of secrets, did you hear about the arrest of Mrs. Greenhow in Washington for spying! Apparently, she's the one who tipped off the Confederate generals at Manassas of the Federals' positions and strength. She is under house arrest with her young daughter. The Richmond ladies, some of whom knew her well from Washington when their husbands were senators and congressmen, are aghast with disbelief. Momma says that wars are times for secrets and intrigue. Momma's right.

Your devoted friend,

Mollie

Washington, D.C.

September 5, 1861

Dear Mollie,

It is strange to see the Rebel flag flying on Munson's Hill, in plain sight of the Federal capital. President Lincoln ordered General McClellan to take command of the Army of the Potomac. This army is in a sad state. For weeks, stragglers sneaked along through the mud trying to find their regiments and the pickets drove in wanderers. Now, General McClellan has the herculean task of reorganizing and disciplining this mass of demoralized men.

The hospitals in Alexandria, Georgetown, and Washington are crowded with wounded, sick, and discouraged soldiers and not enough surgeons or nurses to care for them. The extraordinary march from Bull Run, through rain, mud, and shame, did more to fill the hospitals than the battle itself. The soldiers are sick with measles, dysentery, and typhoid fever.

Some of our men are in grave states of delirium. I was on duty all last night trying to keep John Coles confined to his bed. He would sleep for a while, but then a vivid recollection of the battlefield would come to his mind. He'd sit up in bed, and load and fire his pretend musket over and over again. When we tell him the enemy has retreated, he still wants to pursue them. Throwing his arms around wildly, he shouts, "Come on, men, and fight while there is one Rebel left in Virginia!"

There is so much suffering, but I cannot go among the patients with a long, sad face or intimate by word or look that their case is hopeless. Cheerfulness is my motto. I've noticed that if a man thinks he is a helpless case, then very often, he is. Looking forward to your visit, Mollie.

Your friend,

Frank

Washington, D.C.

September 12, 1861

Dear Mollie,

This letter is being hand-delivered by a good friend. I hope you have recovered from the excitement of our time together yesterday. I should never have let you talk me into it!

Chaplain and Mrs. B. enjoyed our ride together. For a girl who had never been on a horse before, you did quite well with old Ginger. She's an old soul but steady when she pulls our ambulance. I think she was gentle enough for you. Good thing, too, with all the excitement of our journey. Too bad you are not free to share your adventure with your friends at Pizzini's. They would be horrified at best, and at worst, turn you in as a spy!

If only you hadn't said you wanted to see the pickets! Chaplain B. and I rode on ahead to scout for danger as you and Mrs. B. followed not far behind. We never imagined that the pickets would begin to send volleys of Minnie balls across to each other just as we arrived. When the Rebels opened fire, it was just a miracle that we were able to reach cover in the pit.

I think your great-uncle would have had my hide if he had known what we were doing. If he had seen that Minnie ball strike the rail right behind your head, he would have gotten me booted out of the army for sure.

So, how's that for your introduction to my secret life! Want to join up? Would you sign up with the blues or the grays?

I am on duty in the camp hospital for the next few days, but I will try to get away early next week so that we can talk. Would you like to see the rotunda of the Capitol? I can show you around.

Your friend,

Frank

Richmond, Virginia

September 30, 1861

Dear Frank,

Made it home safely. Just wanted you to know. Much to do and can't write now. More later.

Your friend,

Mollie

I hope it worked. Did you have to heat this letter long before the writing on the other side appeared? You are a clever girl, Miss Emma Edmonds—or should I say Private Franklin Thompson—to have thought of this secret way to write. I never knew that soda and water could be used for secret writing! Did the Federals teach you that?

Now you should be free to write me without suspicion as long as the mail posts through Great-Auntie Belle. There is no suspicion aroused by letters to our home from her, and she continues to praise her private courier as exceedingly trustworthy. I will address my letters to Private Thompson and write several lines to "Frank," but my real communication will be on the back using our invisible ink, so that I can speak more freely.

I thought about our talk all the way back on the train to Richmond. You are one amazing girl, Emma Edmonds. I am proud of you. Nothing convinced me more of the rightness of what you are doing than when I went to the hospital with you and saw how the soldiers respect you (or rather, Frank).

I am convinced that it would be wrong to reveal your secret and deprive these men of your faithful service. You can indeed outride, outshoot, and outsmart any of them, and I am proud to be your friend.

It must be difficult to live out this charade though. You explained that you have your own small tent and that you sleep in your uniform for weeks, even months, at a time. Your duties require that you go alone on errands to serve the hospitals and this often gives you some time alone to tend to your bodily needs, such as washing up. But, Emma, I cannot imagine how you have been able to keep up this disguise for all these months.

You are certain the boys in your company don't know. I heard them call you their "little woman" at the hospital, but you said that is because your boots are so small. You clearly have their respect as a soldier so I assume they are simply teasing you for being smaller than most of them.

I've thought about what you told me in Connecticut. We became such good friends, and I could tell you were eager to share your real self with someone. I was glad you confided in me, allowing me to know who you really are and that you had run away, with your mother's help and blessing, from your cruel father.

I wonder how different your life would have been if only you had been able to keep working at the hat shop owned by your mother's friend. If your father hadn't found you, you would not have had to escape to New England. Perhaps, then, your life would have been more normal. Instead, you've had to pose as a boy to be able to keep your independent life as a book salesman and earn a living. And such a good salesman you turned out to be. Mr. Hurlburt raved about you as his finest door-to-door salesman. No wonder he gave you the opportunity to go west to Michigan. You earned it.

I puzzled and puzzled about it on the train, but I realize that just as I am used to moving a certain way to avoid bumping into things with my hoop skirt or catching the angel sleeves of my dress in the fire of a candle, you are accustomed to wearing pants, chopping wood, riding horses, shooting a gun, and holding your own with young Canadian boys: hunting, fishing, or racing horses across open fields and farmlands. Your body is used to moving without encumbrances. Mine is used to living with them. No wonder the Yankee uniform is a relief to you.

You get to ride a horse every day. You have a pistol in your belt. And yet, when you enlisted, the captain assigned you the duties of a field nurse, to work side by side with surgeons in saving lives and relieving suffering. It was as if God knew exactly where he wanted you—with your big heart of compassion and your commitment to tend men's souls as well as their wounds—and he prepared you from childhood for the task.

I now understand your motivation, Emma. And I will support it by keeping your secret—even from the Greats. But, Emma, oh how they would love to know! Three loud hurrahs would be heard throughout Washington as they would marvel at your courage and ingenuity. There is nothing the Greats enjoy more than a good surprise. Perhaps one day you can tell them. I would love to be there if you ever do!

Your friend,

Mollie

Richmond, Virginia

November 1, 1861

Dear Emma,

How do you warm these letters so that you can see the secret messages that are on the other side of my short, and not very interesting, official letters to Pvt. Franklin Thompson? Lanterns? Candles? Do you hold them over the campfire?

Miss Sally Tompkins is now *Captain* Sally Tompkins, Captain in the Army of the Confederate States of America. Ah, ha, Emma Edmonds! You are not the only female in the army. And Miss Sally is an *officer!* So which side is more forward thinking now, Miss Emma? Is it the North with its token disguised private in the Second Michigan Regiment or the South with its publicly proclaimed female captain?

Even Great-Uncle Chester is harrumphing about this one! He, the great champion of women's rights, and the one who takes great pleasure in girls with good heads on their shoulders, doesn't know what to say. I think he just wishes the Northern army had done it first!

The way Charlie explained it to me proves Miss Sally is one smart lady. The Confederate government ordered all private hospitals closed. Only government hospitals can continue to operate. The government couldn't locate its wounded soldiers scattered in so many homes and churches. You mentioned you had the same problem after the Battle of Manassas (I know, you Federals call it the Battle of Bull Run).

Anyway, when Miss Sally got wind of the planned closings, she went to President Davis and spread out all her neatly kept hospital records. She told him that no other hospital sends such a high percentage of soldiers back into active duty than does Robertson Hospital. President Davis couldn't change the order so he had to think of a way around it. He offered to make her an army officer, which would make her hospital an official Confederate army hospital. She willingly took the commission. Momma says that Captain Sally may have accepted the rank of Captain from the government, but she does not accept the pay. Captain Sally pays for all the medicines and supplies herself.

Well, in my opinion, with or without the official title, she has always run this place like a regiment. Clean blankets, clean sheets, clean clothes, are the order of the day. When I volunteer, I help as much with the dressing of the beds as I do with the dressing of the wounds. Captain Sally simply does not tolerate dirt.

All the men love Captain Sally, as they call her. Her care for their bodies is only surpassed by her care for their souls. But, she can be tough. When one soldier decided he was well enough to sneak out for some time in the city, she took away his clothes so he couldn't escape again until he was truly well.

You should have seen Captain Sally today! Robertson Hospital is the Richmond ladies' favorite place to visit. They say they come to volunteer, but none of them has chased any dirt in years. Their servants care for their dresses, their dishes, and their floors. They really don't come to work, but rather to be able to say that they worked. Captain Sally has no patience for those who won't roll up their sleeves. She met the ladies at the door today with aprons, rags, and a list of chores so long, I wonder if we'll ever see them again.

Sissy says she would come and help, but it makes her queasy to see all the wounded men there. She is not so worried anymore about Lemuel because his unit has only seen a small skirmish or two since the big battle at Manassas. She tries to get away to see him when she can.

It seems like things are quiet on both sides now. Perhaps it will stay that way.

The Richmond ladies may adore Captain Sally as our very own Florence Nightingale, but they despise Miss Van Lew's ministrations to the Federal prisoners. Mrs. Adams reported to us at our last sewing meeting that Miss Van Lew continues to bring the Federal prisoners books, food, stationery, and good cheer. She is the only Richmond lady to care for these men. Does that make her evil? These ladies seem to think so. I think not. I think she is courageous.

It takes courage to hold views of the minority at a time when everyone's words and actions are scrutinized. I wish I could speak with Miss Van Lew to know what she thinks about this war. If she chooses to use her funds to help the Federals have more comforts in prison, isn't that as righteous as Captain Sally using her funds to help the Confederate wounded?

Must we turn our backs on all those who are on the other side? Does that mean I should not write to you, or to the Greats? (Of course, not one of the Richmond ladies asks Momma about Great-Uncle Chester since they heard he became a Federal army surgeon. They are horrified, but too polite to Momma to say anything directly to her. I imagine it is spoken about behind her back though.)

This war between the states has drawn a line between North and South. I suppose before it is all over, we will each have to choose. Until then, however, I will stay firmly in the middle.

Your stubborn friend,

Mollie

Washington, D.C.

November 27, 1861

Dear Mollie,

It has been a long time since I have written. My duties at the regiment's hospitals keep me busy. General McClelland has gained command of this great army. You should see the companies of men in full-dress parade. It is a far cry from the panicked army that fled Bull Run. When the time for action comes, we'll be ready.

I volunteered to take your "Greats" to view a skirmish at the pickets, but they declined. Great-Uncle Chester says he prefers stitching men up to watching them blown asunder and Great-Aunt Belle nearly fainted when I suggested it.

Thank you for understanding why I chose to enlist. I suppose because I know what it is like to be in bondage to fear—in my case, fear of my own father—I have sympathies for the slave. Even more, dear friend, I cannot reconcile slavery with what is taught in the New Testament. Enlisting was the best way I knew to do my part for this wonderful country that adopted me and gave me shelter.

Why don't you go to visit the lady you mentioned in your letter, Miss Van Lew? She sounds like she might be an interesting person to know. Would your mother permit it?

Your friend,

Richmond, Virginia

December 26, 1861

Dear Emma,

Such a somber Christmas. At church on Christmas Eve, everyone still called out "Merry Christmas" and "God bless you," but hushed conversations about who has heard what from whom in the field quickly followed. Fathers, brothers, and sons were all missing from the Christmas Eve service. I thought of you, dear friend, and wished you all God's love and protection in these perilous times.

Momma has decided to take in boarders. Sissy and I share a room now and Momma has taken the little room in the back of our house so that she can rent out the front two bedrooms that look out over the city. The mother is nice company for Momma. They have a boy, William, age ten, and a girl, Mary, who is fifteen. And yes, Mary will attend Mrs. Pegram's School. If I sound envious, that's because I am.

Momma is happy about the boarders. If truth be told, we can use the money. With the tightening blockade by the North, prices are skyrocketing. Salt is $1.40 a sack and apples are $20 a barrel. Our Christmas turkey cost us $4.00! Momma says she is going to make it last a week with turkey hash, turkey soup, and turkey fritters.

We did not have our usual Christmas pies and ice cream. Ice cream is up to $9 a quart! I am glad it is not summer or trips to Pizzini's would be out of the question. Maybe Sissy was right to hoard her sugar. Tea is a luxury and coffee is nonexistent. Momma misses her coffee, and Sissy and I miss our tea. A cup of hot tea would be so lovely now. With sugar!

Actually, Sissy used most of her hoarded sugar in a pound cake for Lem for Christmas. She wrapped it with paper and ribbon and sprigs of holly and put it along with four pairs of socks, a woolen scarf, and a jar of pickles in a box to take to Lem. I donated the socks. Sissy's stitching has improved, but she still cannot create patterns with her knitting. All she can do is knit a straight row, and she has not yet mastered one sock.

One night a few weeks ago, Sissy threw down her knitting in frustration, and cried out that she is a failure as a wife. Twisting her hair over and over, she sat there, miserable, staring at me as I worked my knitting needles on which hung a perfect sock.

Momma suggested Sissy make Lem a nice long, straight scarf. Momma, knowing Sissy is such a romantic, told her it would comfort Lem to have a scarf worked with her love to keep him warm in the winter. "Feet are for marching, but necks are for hugging," said Momma knowingly. Sissy threw her arms around Momma and was soon happily clicking along with her needles again. It took Sissy forever to knit the four-foot scarf, but Momma was glad she had something to do to keep her from twisting.

My fingers can knit and purl in their sleep, I suspect. It seems the women and girls cannot speak without the clicking and clacking of needles working their way with the yarn. And yarn, my dear friend! Oh my, is it expensive. There will be no cotton for dresses in the spring either. We hear the Southerners are burning cotton rather than let the Federals get it. I imagine the dress I wear today may be worn a great deal before the war is over, and may ultimately be worn out.

By the way, enclosed is your belated Christmas present. Two pairs of my best work—socks for your "little woman" feet.

It's quiet now as Sissy has gone to visit Lem. Momma and I took our homemade gifts to the soldiers at Robertson Hospital. Captain Sally was most appreciative, but it was the soap Momma made for her that thrilled her the most.

Your friend—especially at Christmas,

Mollie

Richmond, Virginia

December 31, 1861

Dear Emma,

Now I really don't know what I think. Sometimes I lean more toward you and the Greats in this war. Other times, I am ready to enlist myself, but on the side of the Confederates. What I heard today infuriates me.

Mary's family stayed at their home in Alexandria until it was overrun by the Federal soldiers. At first, all they did was take their fruit and vegetables, and their chickens and cows. But when Confederate soldiers made several raids on the railroad near their home, the Federal general ordered all the woods within ten miles of the railroad track to be cut down. Mary's mother begged the captain to leave a few trees around their house for shade, but the soldiers swiftly cut what few trees were left. A few weeks later, their home was confiscated for Federal headquarters. They had one day to pack up to leave.

Mary and her mother quickly hid as many of their valuables as they could. Mary made mortar out of the clay, sand, and lime in her basement and used it to brick up the silver and jewelry into the base of the chimney. She darkened the fresh mortar with soot from the fireplace. Her brother hid things under floorboards and in the attic behind the eaves. Their mother walked around her house, touching furniture, pictures, books, and other things that had been in her family for generations. It was as though she were speaking to each. Saying good-bye.

Maybe I am angry at the Federals. Maybe I am just angry at this whole war. I do not understand the purpose for all the destruction. What is it we are fighting for, anyway? Is it the issue of slavery? Is it land and cotton? Is it the right of the South to govern itself? Or perhaps it is for the freedom to keep others enslaved? It is all so confusing and frustrating.

Grown-ups say Southerners want to choose their own way of life. Last month President Davis told the Confederate Congress: "Liberty is always won where there exists the unconquerable will to be free." But doesn't the slave have an unconquerable will to be free? Don't slaves want to be free of domination and control in the same way that Southern states want to be free of Northern control? So is it the unconquerable will of the North pitted against the unconquerable will of the South? Just who is right? May the best "unconquerable will" win, I suppose.

Emma, you know what you believe and why, and you have committed every resource, skill, and talent you have to what you believe. I, on the other hand, am aimless and drifting. I wish Daddy were still here to talk through these things with me. I wish I could talk this through with the Greats, but Momma says it doesn't look like I can get a pass to see them anytime soon. If I tried to talk to someone here,

Momma says I might be labeled a traitor. It seems it is not permissible to have these kinds of questions right now. At least not right here in the heart of the Confederate government.

Charlie very faithfully comes by each week to read the papers with me. He reminds me he will soon be fifteen and then he is off to join his brother's regiment. I remind him his mother said sixteen is the magic age. He continues to practice with his drumsticks on his nonexistent drum. He says he will be the best drummer the Confederates have ever seen.

Wherever Charlie is, his drumsticks are with him. Momma forbids him to rat-a-tat-tat on our table, but she suffered through his practicing on the railing of our veranda last summer. I don't mind. I understand how Charlie feels. I wish I could do something, too.

Charlie and I get into heated discussions. At times, just for sport, I take the side of the Federals. Charlie leads with his emotions and I with my mind so he always loses the arguments. But if we were scored on passion, he would win. Why is it that I do not care strongly one way or the other about this war? I must not understand it very well at all.

This year is ending, and I am glad. It has been a very troubling year, indeed. I have made myself a promise: If this war continues another year, then I shall make up my mind what I think and why. I am a young lady—nearly seventeen next summer—it is time I know my own mind.

That is my solemn resolution for this New Year.

Your troubled friend,

Mollie

Richmond, Virginia

February 5, 1862

Dear Emma,

On to Richmond! Obviously, we all know that Richmond is the great prize the Federals seek, but that is the last thing I want to hear.

Sissy and I met an interesting new refugee today, Constance Cary. She is staying at the Clifton Hotel with Dr. and Mrs. Fairfax, her uncle and aunt, and her cousins. Emma, I wish I had paid more attention to the painting of Pocahontas that so captivated us when you took me to the rotunda in Washington. When the artist, Chapman, was engaged to paint "The Baptism of Pocahontas" for the rotunda of the Capitol, he asked to paint Constance's mother into his picture as one of the two Englishwomen. So there she is—one of two women standing with their heads wrapped in scarves. They are directly behind the kneeling Pocahontas in the painting. We have to go see it again. Of course, I could not tell Constance that I had just seen the painting in the company of a Federal soldier!

Constance is a different Confederate than I know among my friends here. Her grandfather freed his slaves years ago and made sure that each of his freed slaves learned a trade at his expense so that they could support themselves. Constance does not believe in slavery either.

There must be more to this war than the abolition of slavery. Constance said her family and their friends did not want Virginia to secede from the union, but when Virginia did, they chose to remain loyal. She used to shop in Washington and visit friends. She says it is impossible for her to think of that city as the enemy.

Constance is no stranger to Richmond either. She spent three years here at the boarding school of Monsieur Hubert Pierre Lefebvre. It was there, she said, that she became convinced that slave service did not create the energy of the body or the independence of ideas that she had been taught to value since she was a little girl. Most of the girls from the deepest Southern states who attended school with her had never put on a shoe or stocking for themselves. Can you imagine that? Slave girls attended to their every need. Constance thinks that becoming used to others doing for you creates a laziness of mind and heart.

She told me that if I wanted to read a story of a person with ambition and great heart, I should read about Uncle Tom in the book *Uncle Tom's Cabin*. "But," she said, "be prepared to weep. It will show you full well the curse of slavery on this country." She is a most intriguing girl. She certainly knows her own mind. I wish I knew mine on this issue.

The strangest thing happened this afternoon. The man who delivers our letters and packages asked me if I was a girl who loved to learn. When I acted surprised, he said my great-aunt, on more than one occasion, had mentioned that a package contained books.

He told me that another of his customers in Richmond has a very fine library and he might be able to persuade her to lend me some books. I must have seemed a bit nervous because he left without telling me who this woman is.

I hope he has never opened the packages or steamed open our letters. I continue to address my letters to Private Franklin Thompson. Although my letters to "Frank" are certainly brief, it is my letters written to Emma that no one should see but you. Have you ever noticed anything strange about the envelopes you receive from me?

Your friend,

Mollie

Richmond, Virginia

February 12, 1862

Dear Emma,

Sissy and I spent another amazing afternoon with Constance. When the men in her family left for war, her mother and one of her aunts moved to Culpeper to be near them. "Near, but not idle," Constance said. "Mother nurses each soldier there at the hospital as she would want her son cared for if he were shot."

Constance's brother, only fifteen, decided to join up with the Alexandria Regiment. Constance's mother didn't try to talk him out of it, but she was bound and determined to be as near to him as possible. At the Battle of Manassas, during a pause in the fight, Constance's brother fell asleep under a tree. A mortar shell burst near him without disturbing or awakening him. His captain, seeing the tired little fellow, ran out and picked him up and moved him to safety.

Fearlessness must run in her family. After her mother left for Culpeper, Constance stayed with her two aunts who said they would never leave under any circumstances. Constance admired their grit and determination. "We are not afraid of armies," they said.

And sure enough, they stayed until the Federals arrived to take over their home as an army camp. One day, a Federal officer, according to Constance, quite courteously informed them that they must move and that a war-carriage (that's what Constance calls it—it's really an army ambulance) stood waiting for them at the door.

One of her aunts positively refused to move. She sat there defying them, fire in her eyes, iron in her veins, until two soldiers lifted her, chair and all, and carried her out of the house and put her in the ambulance.

Your friend,

Mollie

Richmond, Virginia

February 22, 1862

Dear Emma,

This morning the man who delivers our packages from Great-Auntie came this time with an extra slip of paper. This was what was written on it:

Miss Elizabeth Van Lew
2311 Grace Street on Church Hill
between Twenty-third and Twenty-fourth Streets

I looked at him in surprise because this is the famous Miss Van Lew that Momma's Richmond kin talk about. She's the one who carries food and sweets and books to Libby Prison for the Federal officers who are imprisoned there. She's the one who the Richmond kin call a Yankee and a traitor.

He simply nodded at me and said, "Her library is superb. She is expecting you. Perhaps you would like to borrow some of her books—perhaps *Uncle Tom's Cabin*." Then he turned on his heels and left without another word. Strange, Emma. Very strange, indeed. This is the same book Constance said I should read sometime. And she is a good Confederate. Why she and her cousins made the Confederate flags that General

Johnson and General Beauregard carry into battle. I don't see what harm it would do to read the book.

Today was the formal inauguration of Mr. Jefferson Davis as president of the Confederacy. Thanks to Dr. Fairfax, we girls viewed the festivities from the galleries of the Capitol and avoided the drenching rain that fell on the crowds. That night, we all went together to the president's mansion. Mrs. Davis was a gracious host and President Davis spoke kindly to all of us. Constance said she has met your President Lincoln in Washington, and that he too is a kind and caring man.

While we were waiting to go inside, Constance introduced us to Hetty and Jenny, her cousins from Baltimore, Maryland. When Maryland did not join the Southern states, they found themselves in a Federal city. That didn't stop Hetty. She took a Confederate banner that had been smuggled through the lines to her, and unfurled it from a window of her home. The Federals took it down and warned her to leave Baltimore or suffer immediate arrest. The two sisters, along with their brother, ran the blockade, carrying drugs for the Confederate hospitals hidden in their birdcage skirts. They also wore new shirts and pants under their dresses for their friends who had enlisted in the Confederacy. Hetty and Jennie laughed to remember how heavy-laden they were with their bottles of quinine and several layers of clothing. Imagine that, Emma!

Your friend,

Mollie

Washington, D.C.

February 26, 1862

Dear Mollie,

Dear friend, a belated thank you. These socks are a most welcome gift—especially with all the drilling we have been doing this cold, snowy, miserable winter. They are on my feet now as I write. General McClelland is determined to make sure we are ready the next time we meet the Confederates. We know we are ready for battle. Each soldier knows it. Yet we wait. After the pitiful showing at Manassas last summer, the boys want to show the Confederates they can fight. There is much grumbling going on in the ranks. If we do not have orders soon, I fear we may have deserters.

Yesterday, we received news of the Union capture of Nashville, the capital of Tennessee. When the announcement was made, the men called out, "Forward to Richmond. On to Richmond." We are desperate to be part of the reclaiming of the Rebel states into the Union, yet we are stuck here in Washington—drilling, drilling, drilling.

The president and Mrs. Lincoln have suffered greatly. Their son, twelve-year-old Willie, died last Thursday from a fever. I wonder if it is typhoid that claims so many lives here.

I did not notice that someone had tried to open our letters. Your great-aunt said to tell you that she has the utmost trust in her courier and that you should trust him, too. These are difficult times, Mollie, but being in the army has taught me one thing. Sometimes you have to just use your instincts to know what to do.

Your friend,

G.

Richmond, Virginia

February 28, 1862

Dear Emma,

President Davis declared today a day of prayer and fasting for the Confederacy. All the girls are making a big show of going without food and attending services at St. Paul's where the president attends.

I respectfully requested they go without me today. I said I wasn't feeling well. But, it could well be that the sick feeling in my stomach comes more from being uncertain about this effort to leave the Union and establish our own country of Southern states. If the Federals are fighting to preserve a union of states that will permit slaves to be free, then perhaps I am more a Federal than a Confederate at heart. But I cannot be a Federal in Richmond.

Charlie came by this afternoon to cheer me up when he heard I was sick. I told him I was feeling better. He spread the newspaper out on the kitchen table. "The paper says here, Mollie," as he began to read, "that 'there is a strong and gallant band of Union men in Richmond willing and anxious to welcome the old flag.' Hmmm. Says here that 'Union ladies are very numerous and they spend their money to help the Federals in Richmond's prisons and hospitals.'"

I immediately thought of Miss Van Lew. If the papers are talking about Union women here in Richmond, they must be speaking about her. According to the Richmond kin, she makes no secret of her leanings toward the North. "Does it say who these men and women are, Charlie?" I asked.

"Nope. Just tells us we better watch out here because this group of traitors is some three thousand persons strong."

I had no idea there were that many people in Richmond who favored the North. I hurried Charlie as he read through the rest of the paper. He was willing to leave soon enough because it was clear I would offer him no food or drink on this fast day. When he left, I put on my cloak and hat and slipped out the back and made my way to Grace Street.

I knocked on the door of the Van Lew mansion set high on one of Richmond's most lovely hills overlooking the city. Miss Van Lew opened the door. No servants or slaves at this house. "Yes?" she asked. I stood there staring at her. She was just as Momma and her kin had described—a small woman with blonde hair and a sharp angular nose. Momma's kin called her "a little bird" and standing there staring at her, I had to agree. This tiny woman could not possibly be a danger to the Confederate cause.

"I'm Mollie Turner," I said as if that should explain it all.

"What can I do for you, Miss Turner?" she replied.

This wasn't going well at all. I was sure the courier who delivered Great-Auntie's packages to me and who delivered mail to Miss Van Lew had spoken to her of me. Why else would he have given me her name and address?

"May I come in?" I asked.

"Certainly," she replied. I quickly stepped inside before she changed her mind. I walked down the hall and noticed her dining room table was set for a celebration. The silver was gleaming and the smells coming from the kitchen were quite pleasant. I think I detected a turkey roasting.

"It's a fast day," I said simply.

"Indeed it is," she replied, "a prayer and fasting day for the success of the Confederacy."

"You're not fasting,"

"No, indeed I am not," she replied.

"Why?"

"I choose not to," she said.

"You're not only *not* fasting; you're having a feast," I said accusingly.

"Hmmm," was all she said in response. She met my gaze coolly, and then continued, "Miss Mollie Turner, what do you think about this Great War? Which side of the war has the most compelling reasons for winning?"

"I'm a Virginian!" I replied as if that answered it all.

"I am, too!" she replied with a smile.

"Virginians must stick with each other . . . and with the Southern states."

"Must we?" she asked.

"Why, of course. It's the right thing to do."

"Why is it right, Miss Mollie?"

I couldn't answer her. The truth is, I can't answer that question for myself. When I turned to leave, she called out, "Just a moment, Mollie." She disappeared for a few moments.

Upon her return, she pressed a book into my hands. "Read this, Mollie. It may help you decide."

I raced down the steps as fast as I could. I did not even look at the book until I had walked three blocks. I was confused, frustrated, angry. At myself mostly. Constance knows what she believes. You know what you believe. The Greats know what they believe. Why, even young Charlie knows what he believes. I, however, have absolutely no idea what I believe about this war and these events that are tearing at the heart of the American people.

After several blocks of walking, nearly running, as fast as I could, I slowed down. A bit dizzy from fasting, I decided to sit down on a bench for a minute. I turned the book over. *Uncle Tom's Cabin.* My heart began racing. How did she know? Had the courier told her after all?

Emma, I feel as though I am being swept up into something much bigger than myself. But perhaps in this way, I will find my own answers.

As always, all of this was written in our special ink. Please destroy this letter after you have had a chance to read it.

Your friend,

Mollie

Richmond, Virginia

March 3, 1862

Dear Emma,

I could not put it down. I read *Uncle Tom's Cabin* in one sitting, just like Constance did. Then I read it again. I have been thinking about it for days. And about what you, the Greats, and so many others believe.

I went back to Miss Van Lew's to return the book. "So soon?" she asked.

"I read it all. Twice. Is it true?"

"This is a novel, Mollie, but Mrs. Stowe based the story on the lives of many slaves. As soon as I read it, I recognized many of the stories I have read. Would you like to read a story written by a slave who escaped his bondage thirty years ago and then helped other slaves escape to Canada?"

I nodded yes and Miss Van Lew motioned for me to follow her. When we came to her library, I gasped. So many books.

Miss Van Lew selected a volume from the shelf and said, "This is my personal favorite. Josiah Henson is a remarkable man. Escaped slave and founder of a community of freed slaves in Canada. He met Queen Victoria in England, you know."

No, I did not know. The man sounded fascinating. I thanked Miss Van Lew and left with another treasure under my arm. I could not wait to get home to begin.

Imagine my surprise when I opened the book and saw that Mrs. Stowe, the author of *Uncle Tom's Cabin,* had written the preface. She recommends this book to all who love the Lord Jesus Christ. She wrote that "whoever thought he would help Jesus, if he were sick or in prison, would help him now by helping the slaves, his afflicted and suffering children."

I raced through the book, putting it down only to weep and pray. This book affected me even more deeply than the first, because Mr. Henson is a real person and his descriptions of all he suffered in slavery are so vivid. After reading his words about all he had gained from freedom, I felt as though I knew him.

Emma, he's an amazing man, who lives now in your native country of Canada. I copied part of his story for you.

I am confused, a Southern girl with Northern thoughts. Emma, I understand your passion now. And the Greats. Is this what Daddy felt, too? Oh, I wish he were here to help me, Emma. He could give me guidance.

Read these pages when you have time. They will astound you.

Your friend,

Mollie

Washington, D.C.

March 6, 1862

Dear Mollie,

I am delighted to tell you that I have been appointed by Colonel Poe to be the regiment's mail carrier. It's a wonderful job, especially now that there are no battles. Nothing delights me more than being the bearer of a letter or package from home. I know the men of Company F quite well, but this job lets me get to know the men in the other companies of our regiment.

Better yet, it means I can be in the saddle most of the day. You know how I love to ride. I enjoy my hospital work, but I miss the wind in my face as I gallop across fields on a good horse.

I learned this week that each side considers it a great success to steal the opposite side's mail. There may be posts or messages of great interest to the other army. This goes for private carriers as well, like the ones your great-aunt uses to get our letters to each other. We must be careful.

Your friend,

Ç.

Richmond, Virginia

March 12, 1862

Dear Emma,

President Davis has declared martial law in Richmond. I'm not sure exactly what that means. I think it means the army rules the city now. Anyway, the army has been going to people's homes at night and arresting them for Federal activities. Some people say they are spies.

The Greats have decided to move Great-Auntie to Baltimore. Washington has become more like a fort, and she misses civilian life. Great-Auntie made all the necessary arrangements with the courier to make sure our letters get to each other. She says we are to trust her courier. He is loyal to the Union and able to move about freely in Richmond. She did not explain more. I'm not sure I want to know more. I am just glad we can write to each other.

Here's some more of Mr. Henson's story I copied for you. I think you'll really like the part when he reaches Canadian land—and freedom.

I went back to visit Miss Van Lew today to talk about some of the things I have been reading. Momma is not sure she approves of Miss Van Lew as a teacher, but then she sees how hungry I am for book learning. Great-Auntie's book packages have slowed down quite a bit these last few months. Momma feels bad that she cannot send me to school, so she has agreed I can borrow books from Miss Van Lew's library. Momma said, "Just be careful not to borrow her ideas, child!"

Sissy is a bundle of nerves as word has come that Lem's unit is preparing for battle. She has taken off again to be near him. I miss her.

Letter paper is becoming increasingly scarce. I am so glad I thought to purchase a supply for our letters long ago when the price was much lower and paper more plentiful.

Your friend,

Mollie

Richmond, Virginia

March 28, 1862

Dear Emma,

I visited Miss Van Lew again. I arrived at her home with the book *Father Henson's Story* in my basket to return to her, and some of the first crocuses of spring as a thank you. Just as I started to knock on the door, she opened it. Miss Van Lew had a basket on her arm and an armload of books. She seemed startled to see me.

"You're on your way out," I said. "I came to return the book. Miss Van Lew, this was an incredible book. I wept and wept. I want to know this man. I feel like I do know this man. It's got me thinking, Miss Van Lew, about a lot of things."

"Child," she said, "I appreciate your enthusiasm, but if you are going to gab at me like that, would you mind helping me out? I see you have a basket there. Would you mind carrying some of these books and accompanying me? We can talk on the way."

"Where are you going?" I asked.

"To Libby Prison. To visit the Federal officers imprisoned there."

I pulled back. It's one thing to borrow literature from Miss Van Lew. It's quite another to assist her in her Federal activities.

"Oh, child, I'm not asking you to come inside with me. Just help me get the books down the hill. It's only four blocks. Not too far out of your way, is it?"

I thought about it a moment. What harm could it do? I'm helping a lady carry books. I'm not aiding the enemy, am I? Or am I?

Emma, you said to trust my instincts and my instincts told me that this was what I should do. Besides, I wanted to talk more about Father Henson and abolition and fugitive slaves. Miss Van Lew was more than happy to tell me what she knew and explained all about something called the Underground Railroad. A lot of Quakers are involved in the Underground Railroad. Because Miss Van Lew went to a Quaker school, she could tell me all about it. I was fascinated with the stories she told. The walk to the prison was much too short.

Miss Van Lew said she would not be long. She was just going to leave these books with the warden. She used to be able to visit with the men, but now that the Northern army is on the move, she is not allowed to speak to them personally. I decided to wait for her. I wanted to learn more about the Underground Railroad.

When she came back, she had armloads of books that the prisoners returned to her. She briefly looked through them and placed some of them in her basket and some in mine. Then we trudged up the hill to her home. When we got to her home, she took both baskets to her library and then returned with mine which now contained a few more books she wanted me to read.

She gave me some biscuits with butter and a tall glass of milk. I looked at her in surprise for eggs, milk, and butter are in such short supply. "I have a farm," she said. As she spread butter on my biscuit and handed it to me, she continued, "It's not too far from the city. When we freed all our slaves, some of them stayed to work the farm—for wages. They are kind enough to bring eggs and milk to Mother and me."

When it was time to go, I turned to Miss Van Lew and said, "You do not seem like a spy to me."

Miss Van Lew laughed and said, "And, what pray tell, does a spy look like, Miss Mollie?"

I fumbled for a few moments, and then said, "Oh, I don't know—sinister, evil perhaps. Anyway, all my Richmond kin say you and your mother are spies. I overheard one lady when we were sewing say that it was not what you took into the prisons that bothered them, it was what you took out."

"Hmmm. Well, Mollie, you were here with me today. What did I take out?"

"Just books, ma'am."

"Yes," said Miss Van Lew in a hushed voice, "but those books might be filled with secrets."

My eyes widened. "Really?" I said.

Miss Van Lew laughed and shooed me out the door, telling me to come back anytime for more books. All the way home, I had to wonder . . . were they?

Your friend,

Mollie

Camp of Company F near Hampton, Virginia

March 29, 1862

Dear Mollie,

We finally got our orders. "On to Richmond!" the boys proclaimed. But, it has done nothing but rain. We march in the rain. We sleep in the rain. We try to cook in the rain—an effort that is made more difficult due to the lack of food. We had two days' rations for marching, but it has been three days since we camped, and the mules pulling the food wagons became stuck in the mud days ago.

We went to houses to ask for food. They gave us bacon, biscuits, pies, and corn bread. When we returned to camp, we smelled the smoke of steak cooking. Someone found a farmer's cow and shot it, and as quick as lightning, had it roasting on the fire. This is exactly the kind of behavior you wrote about, Mollie. But I ask you to consider how men who have been marching for days without food might look at a cow in a field? They do not ask permission. They just take. I'm not saying it is right. I just understand why they are doing it.

I imagine this little town of about five hundred homes used to be quite lovely; but all the houses were burned by order of the Confederate General Magruder. You see, it's not only the Federals who destroy homes and trees. I suppose the Rebels wanted a clearer view of Fortress Monroe that is three miles away. Or maybe it was because the Yorktown road passes directly through the middle. Either way, it is sad to see the burned bricks that used to house families.

Last night, there was a great ruckus at one o'clock in the morning. We left our tents to see what was happening. About forty slaves fell to their knees with hands lifted up to heaven shouting thanks to God and to the soldiers for their deliverance. They fled their homes and made their way through the Rebel lines to the Federal picket line. No sooner had their feet touched Federal soil, than they fell on their knees and shouted "Glory! Glory to God!"

The men and women and children gathered together in a group, praying, singing, and shouting praises. We had a real camp meeting, loud and joyful, as these folks rejoiced. Soldiers brought out coffee, meat, and bread, and built a huge fire as these poor folks were soaked to the bone. Others shared blankets.

There is no sweeter sound to me than the sound of a person tasting freedom for the first time. Mollie, this is why I am fighting in this war. This is why the Union must win. I have read your recent letters and wept with you over Mr. Henson's story. I think you know it, too.

Your friend,

G.

Richmond, Virginia

March 30, 1862

Dear Emma,

I visited Miss Van Lew again. And, again we took books down to Libby Prison. I carried buttermilk and fresh eggs from Miss Van Lew's farm. These she gave as a present to the warden. She is a smart lady. She keeps the guards on her side with sweets and fresh food from her farm, and they continue to let her bring books into the prisons.

I overheard them today as they examined the books, both when she brought them in and when she took them out. They turned them upside down and shook them. They flipped through the pages. I guess they thought letters or secret messages would fall out. But, if Miss Van Lew is a spy, I know she is smarter than that. If there are secrets hidden in those books, they are truly hidden.

However, when she came out of the prison, I noticed that she flipped through the books as well, and carefully placed some of the books in her basket and the remainder into mine. I thought about it all the way back to her house. It was a warm spring day, and we didn't talk much, as we trudged up the hill to her home with our heavy loads.

She gave me her usual treat of biscuit, butter, and milk once the books were put away. Then she brought back my basket filled this time with several new books.

"You are a very fast reader, Miss Mollie. Can you carry all these home today?" I lifted the basket and assured her I could. I asked her for one of the books we had taken from the prison, pretending that I was interested in its topic. She seemed surprised, but went back to the library to get it and added it to my basket.

I hurried home. If Miss Van Lew was getting secret messages from the prisoners in the books, I knew they weren't messages on paper. Unless they were written with a special ink, like ours are.

I heated the book in the oven at low temperatures for a few minutes. I could hardly wait for it to cool. I flipped through the book forward and backward and found not one single word had appeared. I was very disappointed. Well, maybe she is not a spy after all. Or then, maybe she has another way to get messages out of these books.

Your friend,

Mollie

Camp near Yorktown, Virginia

April 3, 1862

Dear Mollie,

It is a great relief to leave that old mud hole we had for our camp. We have had a number of skirmishes and cannon balls and Minnies whiz over us, but no casualties. We prepared the hospital and laid the floors in the hospital tents. But once again, we find ourselves waiting—waiting for battle.

This week, I rode to Fortress Monroe twenty-five miles over muddy roads to pick up the first mail in more than a week. At night, I lay down by my horse to sleep. But after hearing what the other mail carriers at Fortress Monroe had to say, I slept with one eye open. Several soldiers have been robbed and one killed on the same road I had just traveled to get the army's mail. It seems that many on both sides think it's the quickest way to get information about the other. And I thought being the regiment's mail carrier was going to be a relaxing job!

Chaplain and Mrs. B. are still with us. Tonight, Mrs. B. and I decided to visit a community of fugitive slaves near our camp. The men load and unload the military ships that arrive here and the women wash and cook, all for wages now that they are in Federally controlled lands.

I cannot describe the joy of these men and women at being liberated from bondage. There may not be much book learning among these slaves but oh, Mollie, they are deeply knowledgeable about the way of salvation. Mrs. B. and I read to them from the Bible. I wish they could read it for themselves. Yet, many had long passages of the Bible memorized.

Then, one by one, they began to share their life stories, the terror of their time in slavery, the fears suffered after they escaped, the pain of leaving behind those who were dear to them, and the dreams they shared for a life in freedom. Toward the end, one man stood up and said, "I tell you, my brothers, that the good Lord has borne with this here slavery long time with great patience. But now he can't bear it any longer; and he has said to the people of the North, 'Go and tell the slaveholders to let the people go, that they may serve me.'"

Many of the soldiers who were drawn to the meeting by the shouts of praise and the incredible voices lifted up in singing, turned aside lest a fellow soldier see a tear slide down his cheek. Strong men with tender hearts. Men need a reason to fight, Mollie, and there is no greater reason than the freeing of a slave, a man, a brother.

Your friend,

$\mathcal{G}.$

Richmond, Virginia

April 4, 1862

Dear Emma,

I read those books as fast as I possibly could. I wanted to get back to see Miss Van Lew. I couldn't pretend to read them, because she very much wants to know what I think. She asks me lots of questions about each book I read. The Greats would like her a great deal. She will not let me get away with parroting what I have heard my relatives say, neither the Greats nor the Richmond kin. She pushes me to examine what I think.

But mostly, I wanted to try to figure out how she is getting messages in and out of Libby Prison. I am certain that she is. It's my instincts, you know.

But today was not to be one of those days. We didn't go to Libby Prison. I made a great pretense of wanting to see her library so that I could look through many of her books, but I saw nothing out of the ordinary.

One of her freed slaves, Nelson, came from the farm with a basket of eggs. He disappeared into the kitchen for a few minutes and then he came out again. I went back into the kitchen for another glass of milk (Miss Van Lew has told me to make myself at home), and I noticed one egg set off to the side on a plate. The others were in the basket. When I asked Miss Van Lew about it, she looked surprised, and then said, "Never you mind, Miss Mollie. It's just a rotten one, that's all."

I don't think so, Emma. There is something about that egg. There is something about Nelson. I could tell by the way he raised his eyebrows at Miss Van Lew when he motioned to me. She had whispered for him not to worry, but I heard it all. Something is definitely going on here.

Your friend,

Mollie

Richmond, Virginia

April 6, 1862

Dear Emma,

At church this morning, a soldier marched to the front and announced that three trainloads of soldiers who had been fighting in the valley were expected in an hour, and they hadn't eaten in days. Emma, you should see what happens when the Confederate men need food. Confederate women are equal to the task!

All afternoon, hundreds of ladies and their daughters, with aprons covering their Sunday best, marched up and down Main Street and Broad Street. They carried platters piled high with bacon and cabbage, corn pones, sorghum, and brought jugs of Confederate lemonade (vinegar and water since you Federals block lemons from getting to us). Momma, Sissy, and I and our boarders joined the parade and carried trays of what was to have been our Sunday dinner down to the station.

Tattered, bloody, wounded soldiers told us that the Confederacy had half as many soldiers as the Yankees in that battle. How many more of these brave souls must both sides lose before it is over?

Tonight Charlie came over and told me a man by the name of Timothy Webster was sentenced to death for spying for the Union. He used to take letters and packages from Richmond to Baltimore, including important information from the Confederate generals. When he got there, he'd open them, copy the important sections, and send the information on to Washington. Emma, do you think our letters are ever opened? What do we know of our mail courier? I know Great-Auntie trusts him, but many people trusted Timothy Webster, too.

Folks are shocked. No one suspected him at all. What will they think now of Miss Van Lew? They already suspect her of Union sympathies. What now?

Your friend,

Mollie

Richmond, Virginia

April 10, 1862

Dear Emma,

Miss Van Lew seemed quieter today on our way to Libby Prison. Of course, I chattered away as usual. There are so few people I can have these discussions with. But,today, Miss Van Lew seemed a bit anxious. I wonder if it is because of Timothy Webster.

We left books and took back others, as usual. This time she did not flip through them as was her custom, but simply loaded up both our baskets and hurried back to her home. When we arrived there, Nelson met her, wearing a worried look. They disappeared for a few minutes in the library.

When she returned, Miss Van Lew suggested that I leave. No biscuit. No milk. No new books. When I reminded her that I needed a new book to read, she pulled one from her basket and slipped it into mine. With apologies and excuses about not feeling well, she hurried me out the door.

I thought about it all the way home, Emma. Something is definitely up in that house. This seems to be a time of secrets. Your secret. The secrets of spies. Secret hiding places for Confederate valuables. The secrets I am sure Miss Van Lew has hidden in that house.

Do you have other secrets, Emma? Secrets you are not telling me? We spend our time at St. Paul's now sewing bandages and sandbags to fortify the city. Does that mean the battle lines are drawn at our city gates? The ladies said that President Davis might send his family further south. It certainly makes you wonder how close Richmond is to destruction.

Tonight, Momma had Sissy and me pull up the floorboards in the attic and hide our family silver. More secrets.

Your friend,

Mollie

Richmond, Virginia

April 21, 1862

Dear Emma,

General Magruder marched thousands of his men through the streets of Richmond yesterday! From early in the morning until evening, the marchers continued through the city cheered on by the crowds, the drummers, and lively tunes played by the military bands. From every window, smiling girls waved handkerchiefs and cheered the men. Joy and celebration and sadness and tenderness all in one day, all in one street. Wives, children, and sisters looked for husbands, fathers, and brothers. If only a moment could be granted for a quick good-bye. A touch of the hand. A kiss. So many tears. So many fears.

Great-Auntie is concerned for Mother, Sissy, and me. She wants us to come to Baltimore to stay with her. Momma is frightened, I can tell, but refuses to leave the home she had with Daddy.

This afternoon, Momma asked me to take the silver candelabra up to the attic to find a suitable hiding place. Sissy and I had already worked up all the loose boards for the other silver we hid, so there didn't seem to be much hope in storing them underfoot. I looked around the attic and saw a bit of fabric poking out from behind a rafter in the roof. I stood a few boxes on top of each other, and pulled at the edge of the fabric behind the rafter. It wouldn't budge. I pulled harder, and to my great surprise, a packet of letters fluttered down from the rafter. They had been wrapped up in a handkerchief—one of Daddy's handkerchiefs!

My heart beat quickly as I gathered the letters. I put the handkerchief up to my face and felt its softness. I began to cry. I miss my daddy so terribly much. All of his women—Momma, Sissy, and I—have tried to be so brave during this unsettling time, but I know we all wish Daddy with his quiet strength was present with us now.

There were three letters. One addressed to Momma, one to Sissy, and one to me. I carefully placed Momma's and Sissy's letters on a box, and sat down on the other box with Daddy's letter in my hand. Why had he written them? And why had they been hidden, in the rafters of the roof, where we were very much unlikely to ever find them.

I carefully opened his letter to me. It was written in 1859, six months before he died. I have copied it for you.

Dearest Mollie,

   If you are reading this letter, then the great war I feared would come upon this country has begun. Perhaps you are in the attic hiding valuables. Perhaps even you, your sister, and your mother have had to hide in the attic. My guess is that you, Mollie, found these letters. You were always the most observant of us all. Ever since you were a young child, you watched and waited, observing, learning, calculating, taking it all in. Only then would you venture to act.

   My dear Mollie, these are perilous times, and you have been placed in these times for a reason. I have been spared the pain of going through them. If you are reading this letter, then I am now safe with our Lord. Yet even now, I can see that troubles are upon us. This is why I am writing to you a special letter that is meant for your eyes alone.

   I too am observant, Mollie, and I have seen how you have leaned into the thinking of the Greats, as you dearly love to call them. You know I was raised with their thinking as well, and I know you often wondered what I thought about slavery, abolition, and the views that divide our great country. Because of my love for your mother, I never voiced my views in our home, but it is time now for you to know them.

   Mollie, I cannot reconcile slavery with my beliefs in a loving God who would give the life of his Son for *every* man. Slavery states that a certain class of men, women, and children do not deserve freedom. To call someone a slave is to label that person as property, just as you would a wagon. But an enslaved person has a soul. An enslaved person has a heart beating in his breast for freedom. God designed all people that way—to love liberty and freedom. Otherwise, we would not recognize our own bondage to sin and our need for freedom in Christ.

If you are reading this letter, in the midst of a great war over the issue of slavery and other issues that divide the North from the South, I imagine you have wondered many times what I would have done if I had lived to see this day. From this vantage point, I cannot say much about what is going on in your life now. It has likely been years since these words were written. At least, I hope the conflict stays away that long. But, Mollie, if you find yourself wondering what your father would have done, ask yourself this—what would you do? What would you risk in this war for your beliefs?

Know that your father loves you more than he can bear. As I write this, I fight back the tears that threaten to wash away these words. I want to be healed, but if I am not, and I go to be with the Lord, know that I am proud of you and love you very much. As Uncle Chester says, "Mollie, you have a good head on those pretty shoulders of yours." Yes, Mollie, you have a good head and a good heart. Use them wisely. Pray often. The Lord will show you what to do.

With all my love,
Daddy

I let the letter fall to the floor and buried my head in my hands and sobbed. When all was spent inside me, I brushed the final tears from my face and lifted my apron to dry my eyes. I picked up the letter and read it again and again. Then I took the other two letters to Momma and Sissy. Emma, it was a sad and happy day in our home. We slept with Daddy's letter to each of us tucked under our pillows that night.

Your friend,

Mollie

Richmond, Virginia

April 30, 1862

Dear Emma,

They hanged Timothy Webster yesterday. He was part of the Secret Service and spied on the Confederates for the Union. Charlie came by to tell me all about it. He'd read about it in the papers. Spying is dangerous business, Emma.

Throngs of families are leaving Richmond. The call for women to sew thousands of sandbags to fortify the city frightens many. Great-Auntie begs us to secure passes to visit her. Momma says we will stay here no matter what. Momma keeps Daddy's letter with her at all times. I don't know what it said, but she is calmer now and stronger.

Sissy is also determined to stay, that is until she learns where Lem's unit will be. With all we have heard about the advancing Northern troops, I think even she will stay put.

I have not seen Miss Van Lew in several weeks. So much has been happening that I haven't had much time to read either. Last night, I pulled the book she gave me out of my basket. The title surprised me. It was a medical book on fevers. I remembered how distracted Miss Van Lew was that day and realized she must have put the book in my basket by mistake. I decided I would take it back to her.

As I turned to place the book back in the basket, I noticed something strange about the spine. When I turned the book and held it up to the light, I saw a faint impression. Could there be something hidden in the spine of the book? I took a knife and very carefully pulled the spine away from the book. A small piece of paper fell out. It was two inches by two inches with writing on it that made no sense to me at all. It looked like some kind of cipher or code. I copied it down on another sheet of paper. Then I put it back in the spine of the book and put the book in my basket.

I started out the door, but instead of turning left toward Miss Van Lew's, I turned right. I kept walking not really knowing where I might end up. I had to think. What would I say to Miss Van Lew when I returned the book? Should I let her know that I found the coded message inside? Was it important? It's been a whole month, so surely the message it contained for the Federals would be long out of date. Perhaps it is best, I reasoned, not to say anything at all.

I walked and walked for two hours. Finally, I realized I had come to the cemetery where Daddy is buried. I found his grave and sat down in the fresh spring grass. Like Momma, I keep Daddy's letter with me at all times. I pulled it out of my pocket and read it again. This time, something jumped out at me. Daddy had told me what he thought about slavery, and I agreed. But Daddy had not told me what he would do about it. Would he be like Constance and her family and still fight for the Confederacy even though they abhor slavery, or would he have found himself on the side of the Federals?

I realized it was not so important that I know what he would do. It was more important that I decide what I would do. And what would I do with this information I had found? Spy fever is very hot here in Richmond right now. Just take this book to the authorities, and Miss Van Lew would no longer be in business.

I jumped up, brushed off my skirt and began the long walk to Miss Van Lew's home. When I got there, I found she had just gotten home from a visit to Libby Prison.

"Come in, Miss Mollie. I've been wondering when you would come for more books." She opened the door wide and ushered me into her parlor. "Would you care for some milk and biscuits, Mollie?"

"Not today," I answered. "I came to return a book—a book I don't think you meant to give me."

Miss Van Lew looked at me quizzically and then glanced at the title of the volume I had placed in her hands. She quickly looked at me again. I remained stone-faced, though I saw her run her fingers along the spine. *She knows*, I thought.

"You brought this book back to me, Mollie. Why?"

"To return it, of course, and get another," I replied.

"This book is different," she said.

"Oh yes," I laughed. "I think it is something my great-uncle Chester might like to read. He's a doctor, but I have no interest in a book on fevers, Miss Van Lew."

"Hmmm."

"My great-uncle Chester is a surgeon with the *Union* army," I added.

Miss Van Lew looked at me in surprise. "Really?"

"Yes, he and my great-aunt believe I have a good head on my shoulders."

"That you do, Miss Mollie. And what did you think of this book?"

"Oh, I didn't read it, Miss Van Lew. As soon as I touched it and read the title on the spine, I knew that this book was not meant for me."

"Hmmmm," said Miss Van Lew. She turned toward the window, hugging the book to her chest. She seemed to be thinking very hard. After a few minutes, she twirled around, and said, "I think I have another book that might interest you." She walked to the library and came back with a book on codes and ciphers used in previous wars. "Why don't you take this book and see if you find anything in it that interests you."

Curious, I took the book and placed it in my basket and bid her a good day. There was much we had said to one another, and much we had left unsaid. We were playing a cat and mouse game. I wanted to see if she is a spy. She wanted to see if I can be trusted.

I went home that night and read through the book on ciphers and codes, alongside the coded message I had copied. I'm good in mathematics, but I found it hard going. After midnight, I gave up and turned down my light.

Your friend,

Mollie

Richmond, Virginia

May 5, 1862

Dear Emma,

I have been hard at work for days now trying to crack this coded message. I cannot do it. I am convinced Miss Van Lew has a special cipher for the message—maybe it is one she made up herself. I have decided I will not turn her in. Somehow I have to make her understand that.

I took one of the more simple codes I found in the book and created my own secret message. This is what it said, "You can trust me. I want to help." When I put it in code, it read:

WGS ACL RTSUR KG G UCLV RQ FGJR

I folded the small slip of paper carefully, slit open the spine of the book, and tucked the message inside. If she is a spy, she will look there, and she will know how to unscramble my message.

Once again, I was off to Grace Street with a book in my basket. I knocked on the door and Miss Van Lew answered the door. "Mollie!" she exclaimed. "Back so soon? The book was that easy to read?"

I came in and said, "Oh, no. I found it fascinating, but I imagine that all the codes one might have for a secret message are not contained in this book."

"Probably not," she agreed. I saw her finger the spine, almost unconsciously, when I gave her the book. She put it down on the table by us and said, "Mollie Turner, there comes a time in everyone's life when they must determine what risks they are willing to take for what they believe. Father Henson did that when he ran away with his family. They could have been captured. Imprisoned. Even killed."

Somehow I knew she wasn't talking about runaway slaves. I think she was trying to tell me about herself. She was so cryptic though. I had to think hard to stay with her as she continued to talk.

"And like Father Henson, he was never sure who he could trust. Who might he depend on to help him with his plans to get his slave family to freedom forever? At points of great necessity, like when he needed food for his family or passage across the river, he revealed who he was or what his purposes were. Sometimes, he had to judge the character of a man or a woman . . . or a girl . . . to determine if he could trust her. Sometimes, by depending on a few good-hearted souls, he was able to secure his highest hopes. Life is like that."

All right, I said to myself. She is talking about us. She wants to know if she can trust me. More cat and mouse games. She is wondering if her judgment of my character is accurate. I understand. One false move and her whole enterprise will come crashing down. Just look at Mr. Webster. He got away with spying for the Union for a long time, but then one person revealed his secret.

I stood to leave. "Thanks for the book, but I think there is much more you could teach me than what is contained in that book." And then I left.

I understand her caution, but now that I am ready, I wish she would trust me. Emma, I want to help the Union any way I can. I don't think this friendship with Miss Van Lew came by accident.

I haven't heard from you in a long time. I can tell from the preparations here in the Confederacy that you too may have very little time for writing. Know that I pray each day for your safety, dear friend.

Your friend,

Mollie

Camp near Yorktown, Virginia

May 15, 1862

Dear Mollie,

The two letters I enclosed in this envelope are ones that I wrote to you last month and kept hidden until now. I could not send them until I knew for certain that you are committed to the Union. Not until you said it with your own handwriting was I willing to risk sharing my new duties with you. You were trustworthy, Mollie, with my secret of enlisting in the army, and you have been faithful all these months. But, in this war, we cannot be too careful. With my new responsibilities, I had to be sure.

Take care, dear friend.

E.

Camp near Hampton, Virginia

April 6, 1862

Dear Mollie,

Sorry for such a brief letter on the other side, but when you read this long letter in our secret ink, you will know my reason for caution. I wrote it today, but will hold on to it until I can be certain of your commitment.

Chaplain B. said he knew of a situation he could get for me if I had sufficient moral courage to undertake its duties. This morning, a detachment of the Thirty-Seventh New York rode out as scouts and brought back several Rebel prisoners. One of them reported that a Federal spy, a Secret Service agent, had been captured in Richmond. Chaplain B. said the Union army needs a replacement for this spy to get important battle plans and information to our generals. "However," he said, "it is a situation of great danger and vast responsibility."

I told Chaplain B. I would think and pray about it. I rode off alone for a few hours to consider the task. Was I capable of performing the duties of a spy with honor and excellence? I certainly knew how to fool people with a disguise! I have been doing that now for several years, both with civilians and now in the army.

I ride hard and fast. I am quick and clever. I am observant and have a good memory. I think I can take any hardship that might be required.

And I do not worry for my life. I leave that in the hands of my Creator, feeling assured that I am just as safe passing through the picket lines of the enemy, if it is God's will that I should go there, as I would be in my tent in Federal camp. And if not, then his will be done.

I rode back to speak privately with Chaplain B. Yes, he could submit my name to headquarters as a willing volunteer for this duty.

Your friend,

C.

Washington, D.C.

April 7, 1862

Dear Mollie,

General McClellan, General Heinzelman, and General Meagher interviewed me at General McClellan's headquarters for the position in the Secret Service. I answered all their questions truthfully. They assumed, of course, I was who I appeared to be—Franklin Thompson, the private of Company F, Second Michigan Volunteer Infantry Regiment.

When they examined my ability with firearms, I passed with flying colors. (I told you I can outshoot any soldier!) Finding me fit for the assignment, they administered the oath of allegiance to the Union, which I proudly affirmed. The generals complimented my faithful service to the Union so far, and Chaplain B. could not have been prouder.

With only three days to prepare for my debut as a spy, I may not be able to write for a while. I have to admit, Mollie, these new duties in the Secret Service of the United States government are exactly what I was meant to do. I can feel it. I am sure to have some grand adventures. I hope I do not run out of our special ink so I can write you all about them!

Your friend,

E.

Richmond, Virginia

May 20, 1862

Dear Emma,

What a strange and wonderful day. The courier who delivers our mail brought a huge packet of your letters. I took time to read each one, and especially the last two letters about your new duties. The courier also had a book for me. It was wrapped in brown paper and tied with string. I thought it was from Great-Auntie until I opened it. It was the same old book on codes and ciphers.

I took it to my room and looked for the slit in the spine. There I found a small piece of paper with a coded message. It looked to be the same code I used before. I unscrambled the words and read: "Come to Grace Street. I do trust you."

I quickly gathered my basket and put the spine of the book back together. When I got to Miss Van Lew's house, she greeted me with a plate of biscuits and butter and a glass of cool buttermilk. But I was too excited to eat.

"I pondered it for many nights, Miss Mollie. You could have turned me in. Instead, you returned my book with the message safe inside. You are a clever girl, and you found a simple way to let me know that you knew I was passing on messages from the Federal prisoners at Libby Prison to the Federal government. You also found a way to let me know you want to help.

"Are you sure, Mollie? Are you sure you want to get involved in this? I know I am watched. I am sure they have seen your comings and goings here as well and I would never want you to be in danger."

I told her that I wanted to do all I could to bring this war to an end as quickly as possible and to bring this country—a country where all people can be free—back together again.

"Mollie, I'm not sure it will be that easy," she replied, "but every person has a role to play in this great conflict. I cannot sit idly by. I sensed from the moment I met you that you could not either. Are you ready for your first assignment?"

I nodded yes. "The code I use is not one in these books. You were smart enough to figure that out. I will not give you the cipher to it either. We will make up a special code just for the two of us to use. Sometimes you will carry messages that you will not be able to decipher. That is best for your safety.

"Just like today," she continued, "the courier will bring you a book." When my eyes widened with disbelief, she added, "Yes, the man your great-aunt selected is part of our group. He can be trusted. Check the spine of the book for the messages. Your job will be to get it to the next relay station. I am constantly watched. You will be a big help."

"Who is the next person I take the message to?" I asked.

"There will be two coded messages in the spine of the book. One will be the message you are to carry. The other will be our own code, one that only the two of us have the cipher for. That is where you will get the information for the person who is to take the message next."

We sat there for another hour, working out our own code and cipher. I can tell no one, not even you, dear Emma. But I am sure you understand.

Before I left, Miss Van Lew explained that I might notice her beginning to act a bit strangely. "Mollie, the folks in Richmond already think I am off my rocker because of my Union views. Why not take it a bit further? Why not let them think I have gone completely crazy? Do not be surprised by what you see me do or say. But, Mollie, it will not do for you to come by the house anymore. My demise into insanity should be a good cover for your staying away. The books will come to you like today by the trusted mail courier, so it is just as likely they came to you from your great-aunt."

"But, Miss Van Lew, I so enjoy our talks and our times together. I don't want them to end. I have learned so much from you."

"Oh, child, they are not over. They are just postponed for a bit. We will have times like this again. The Union must survive, and when it does, we can talk again. Until then, it is safer for you to stay away. Besides, once you see Old Crazy Bet, your mother will not want you here again!"

We laughed and I hugged her good-bye. This time, I only left with a biscuit in my basket.

Your friend,

Mollie

Near Williamsburg, Virginia

May 21, 1862

Dear Mollie,

I received word of my first mission just a few weeks after I was commissioned into the Secret Service. I went to Fortress Monroe, where I purchased a suit of clothing, plantation style, so I would appear to be a hard-working slave. Then I had the barber shave my hair close to my head. I colored my head, face, neck, hand, and arms dark with silver nitrate and put on a wig of black hair.

I put a few hard crackers in my pocket and with my revolver loaded and capped, I started out on foot at dusk without a blanket or anything that might create suspicion. About 9:30 that night, I passed through the outer picket line of the Union army. By midnight, I crept past a sentinel and got within the Rebel lines. I went on a safe distance from the picket lines and lay down and rested until morning. Notice that I said I rested. I surely didn't sleep. My heart was pounding too loudly.

The next morning, I met a group of slaves carrying coffee and food to the Rebel pickets. They gave me a cup of coffee and a piece of corn bread. The slaves reported to work on the Rebel fortifications. I followed and watched them as they worked. One of the officers came up to me and said, "Who do you belong to, and why are you not at work?"

"Name's Ned. I'm free and goin' to Richmond to get some work."

The officer shoved me and said to the foreman, "Take that rascal and set him to work. If he don't work well, tie him up and give him twenty lashes. That'll teach him that there's no such thing as free slaves here!"

I joined about a hundred other slaves, who were building the fort. I took a pickax, shovel, and wheelbarrow and did whatever my companions in bondage did. The portion of the parapet that I was building was eight feet high. With the help of another slave, I wheeled gravel in the wheelbarrows to the top of the parapet. I worked until my hands were blistered and raw. But, as I worked, I kept my eyes and ears open.

When night came, they let us roam around the fortifications. Then I made a sketch of the outer works of the fort and a list of all the guns I saw that night. I put both papers in the inner sole of my shoe and returned to the slave quarters. I knew I could not shovel or carry wheelbarrows the next day with my blistered hands. I found a lad about my own size who had been carrying water, and paid him to swap places with me for the next few days.

The second day was much easier. During my water-carrying duties, I learned the number of reinforcements that arrived from different places and even saw General Robert E. Lee. I carried water to my slave friends. One of them looked at me strangely and said, "Jim, I think that fella is turning white!" My heart raced, but I made a joke, and they laughed at me. I got off by myself as soon as I could to take out my small pocket looking glass. Sure enough, I was getting lighter. I took my small vial of silver nitrate and applied some more of it to prevent the remaining color from coming off.

On the third day as I filled the soldiers' canteen, I heard a familiar voice. It was the peddler who used to come to our Federal camp and headquarters once each week with newspapers and stationery. Now, here he was with the Rebels, giving them a full description of our camp and forces! He also brought out a map of the entire placement of General McClelland's positions! He was a traitor. I had to get back!

That night I slipped noiselessly through the woods to the picket line. I gave the familiar signal to our pickets, and they let me through the Federal lines. I went straight to General McClelland's headquarters, presented my report, and received the hearty congratulations of the General himself!

It was a great day, Mollie. My slave costume was put away for another day and my Frank costume was put back on. Only you, Mollie, know me as Emma. I'm glad someone knows my true self.

I had to postpone my second visit into enemy territory. On May 5th, General Hooker attacked the Rebels near Williamsburg and the Second Michigan was ordered there as reinforcements. We marched eight miles in the drenching rain. The fighting was fierce and many of our own were wounded. I worked for days with the surgeons. After the battle, we moved as many as we could to the churches and college buildings in Williamsburg.

So many young men wounded and dying. Time after time, I would sit at the bedside of a young man who, knowing he was dying, would ask for the chaplain and then give a strong statement of his faith in Jesus Christ. So often, the message was this: "Tell Mother that Christ does not desert the dying soul." "Tell Mother I died believing in Jesus." That is our only comfort, isn't it in perilous times like these—that because of Jesus, we will see each other again one day?

Your friend,

$\subsetneq$.

Richmond, Virginia

May 22, 1862

Dear Emma,

It was not long before the first book arrived. It came just like Miss Van Lew said it would, wrapped in brown paper and tied with string. The courier gave it to me with a letter from Great-Auntie and several letters from you.

I took the package to my room and opened it. Inside the spine of the book, I found the coded messages. One I could not decipher. I laid the other side by side with my code, and unscrambled the message. It gave me the name of a clerk in a store a few blocks away and the code word "peaches." I assumed he was part of Miss Van Lew's relay network to get messages through to the Federal lines.

A few hours later, I left the house with the coded message folded up in a hollowed out acorn with the top securely back on. The acorn felt like a brick in my pocket. I thought everyone I passed knew what I was carrying. When I got to the store, I asked Mr. Simpson if he had any peaches. He looked up, surprised. My heart started beating quickly. Of course, this isn't peach season. Maybe I had unscrambled the message wrong. My face flushed hot, and my heart pounded in my chest.

"I think I have a jar back here, young lady. Follow me." When we got to the back of the store, I took the acorn out of my pocket and started to hand it to him. He pointed to a peach pit pin on his watch chain and turned away. Miss Van Lew warned me about this. The peach pit was carved like a clover. If my contact held the clover down, then it was safe to talk. If he held it up, we were to go our separate ways. He held it up. It was not safe to talk. My eyes darted around the store. A man watched us over his newspaper. My right hand gripped the acorn in my pocket so tightly that I thought it might shatter. I stuffed the acorn back in my pocket, turned on my heels, and called out, "Oh well, I guess I'll try another day. Momma did so want a taste of pickled peaches for her supper tonight."

When I got outside, I practically ran down the block. I was so frightened that I gasped for air. What should I do? Now I had a message that needed to be delivered and my contact told me I couldn't leave it. How would I know when I could come back?

I walked a few more blocks and then turned back for home. When I got within a block of the store again, a kindly old man walked up to me with a flower. "A pretty flower for a pretty girl with a good head on her shoulders?" I gave a start. Was this a secret message? How odd! I took the flower and scrutinized the old man. But he just passed on and gave another flower to the next girl and said the same thing.

I kept jiggling the acorn in my pocket. This was simply not going to work. I made my way back home and sat on the veranda puzzled and confused. It was a hot day. How I longed for lemonade. One day, when this cruel war is over, I will drink gallons and gallons of lemonade—with lots of sugar. A lady walked by and said, "You look miserably hot, my dear. Please take my fan." I protested, but she insisted, and handed me her straw palm fan.

I fanned myself with the fan over and over. It did feel good. Suddenly, I sat up straight in the rocking chair. The fan had writing on it. Gibberish. Letters strung together that made no sense. I dashed inside to my room and pulled out my code from its secret hiding place. Laying the code next to the fan, I unscrambled the message. This one read: Capitol Square.

This spying business is exhausting. I ran out of the house and walked as quickly as possible to Capitol Square. It was crowded today with lots of women and girls admiring the flowers. The fan came in handy since it was quite warm. It seemed strange to me that I should bring my secret message right here to the grounds of the Confederate government. A lovely woman that I had not seen before in Richmond approached me. "It's a gorgeous day, isn't it?"

I was quite wary of her. "Yes, lovely." I continued to fan myself with the fan.

"It's hard to believe fall will be right around the corner. Nothing like a gorgeous fall day with the tall oaks dropping their little acorns all around. You see that oak there? It's my favorite one."

I couldn't tell if this was a message or not. It sure was strange. I watched until she walked away. Then I thought I would try an experiment. I walked over to the tree and slipped the acorn down between two roots of the tree. I walked away casually but stood near enough to watch. Sure enough, several minutes later, the lady came back and sat down under the tree pretending to read a book. But I saw her gently pick up the acorn and put it in her pocket. After fifteen minutes, she stood up to leave.

This spy business is complicated. When I got home, Momma said I had a message from the store that my pickled peaches were in. What! Had I just left the acorn message with the wrong person? I thanked Momma, who looked very puzzled, and ran down to the store. Mr. Simpson had his peach pit pin turned the other way. He gave me a jar of pickled peaches to take home and said he wanted me to know the secret message was safely on its way. It turns out the lady who gave me the fan is his wife, Mrs. Simpson. The lady I met in the park, the one who took the acorn is his daughter. They all help with taking the messages to the next station.

I will be happy if it is weeks before I have another message to send on up the lines!

Your friend,

Mollie

Near the Chickahominy River

May 23, 1862

Dear Mollie,

We camped along the Chickahominy River waiting for the men to finish the bridges across the river. I got my second assignment to see what I could learn about the enemy's troops and weapons. After the battle in Williamsburg earlier in the month, I bought a dress of an Irish peddler woman. Imagine that now, Emma the girl, disguised as Frank the boy, disguised as Bridget the Irish peddler woman.

I packed my disguise in a pie basket and swam my horse across the river. Then, I gave him a farewell pat, and let him swim back again to the other side, where a soldier waited for his return. It was now evening. I didn't know the exact distance to the picket line, but I thought it best to avoid the roads. I slept in the swamp that night.

It took me some time to get my disguise right. I put on the river soaked dress and hid my uniform in the woods. The food I had carefully packed in the basket was wet and rotting. I certainly looked like a brokenhearted forlorn Bridget who should never have left Ireland. After several hours traveling in the swamp, and trying out my Irish brogue on the birds and the squirrels, I saw a small white house in the distance.

I thought it was deserted, but when I came inside, I saw a sick Rebel soldier, lying on a straw mattress on the floor. Assuming my Irish brogue, I asked him if I could help. Ill, with typhoid and barely alive from the last skirmish with the Federals, he spoke in a whisper. He had crawled on his hands and knees to take refuge in this deserted house.

I kindled a fire, found some flour and cornmeal, and baked a large hoe cake. I heated some water for tea, and fed the poor famished Rebel as tenderly as if he had been my brother. He thanked me with as much politeness as if I had been Mrs. Jefferson Davis. I longed to restore him to health and strength, not considering that the very health and strength I wished to secure for him would be used against the Union.

When he rallied, we spoke for a while. He was a Confederate soldier, but I saw no hatred of the Yankees in him. I asked if he was a soldier of the Cross. He replied with enthusiasm. "Yes, thank God! I have fought longer under the Captain of my Salvation than I have under Jeff Davis."

Then I asked him, "Can you, as a disciple of Christ, conscientiously and consistently uphold the institution of slavery?"

He made no reply but his face fell, "Oh Bridget, you have touched a point upon which my own heart condemns me." We talked a bit more, but he was failing fast.

I found a little bit of salt pork and cornmeal and made gruel for my patient, but he barely swallowed it. "Dear Bridget, tell me true, am I dying?"

"Yes, my new friend, you are dying. Have you made your peace with God?"

He sighed and then whispered, "My trust is in Christ. He was mine in life, and in death he will not forsake me." I leaned close, and he asked me to find the Confederate camp between here and Richmond and let Major McKee of General Ewell's staff know what had happened to him.

I held him until he struggled in his breathing. He gained some strength and whispered, "Glory to God. I am almost home!" He labored a few hours more, and then, in my arms, he slipped away to heaven. I thank God, Mollie. It was my privilege to be there. I knew God had led me to that deserted house so he would not die alone.

The next morning, I found a number of articles that helped me perfect my disguise: mustard, pepper, an old pair of spectacles, and a bottle of red ink. With the mustard powder, I made a strong plaster and tied it on my face until it blistered thoroughly. I then covered the blistered face with court plaster. With ink, I painted a red line around my eyes, as if I had been crying. I put on the green glasses and my Irish hood, which covered about six inches of my face. I filled my baskets with other items in the house that an Irish peddler woman might be expected to have. Then I buried my pistol and anything else that might create suspicion.

After I had walked five miles, I saw the Rebel sentinel ahead. I sat down to rest and steady myself for this interview. I took the black pepper from my basket and sprinkled some of it on my handkerchief, and applied it to my eyes. Looking in the mirror, I saw a sad, sad lady indeed. When I met the guard, I told him my sorrowful story of running away from the Yankees. I lifted my peppery handkerchief to my eyes until tears ran down my face in steady streams. With my best Irish brogue, I sobbed my miserable story, and the guard let me pass on my way to the Rebel camp.

Once at the camp, I easily overheard news of the enemy's troops—both their position and their strength. Everyone was talking about the upcoming battle. I had plenty of information and needed to get back to the river, but I had a duty to perform for a brother in Christ, even if he was an enemy in this war.

I went to the headquarters and asked for Major McKee. In my best Irish brogue, I told him the story and delivered the soldier's watch and his letters. I didn't need the black pepper to help me cry as I thought about this man.

Major McKee rose to his feet and said, "You are a faithful woman, and you shall be rewarded. Can you direct the men to that house to show them where Captain Hall's body is?" When I nodded yes, he gave me a ten-dollar greenback, saying as he did so, "If you succeed in finding the house, I'll give you more."

I thanked him but wouldn't take the money. He looked at me suspiciously, for why would a poor old beggar woman not take whatever money she could get? I was scared, Mollie. I thought I might have blown my cover. Suddenly, I burst into a passionate fit of weeping, "Oh Major, forgive me. My conscience would never let me take money for carrying a message that the boy is dead. Oh, my, I could never do such a terrible thing." He seemed satisfied, and when he returned with his men, I begged him for a horse to ride, saying that I had been sick for several days.

I rode at the head of the band of Rebels as a guide. The Rebels wished they had brought an ambulance, but I thought this better suited my plan. The men went into the house and brought out Captain Hall's body on a stretcher. The sergeant asked me to ride down the road a little way and if I saw any Yankees to ride back as fast as possible and let them know. I happily complied with the first part of his request. I rode down the road slowly, and not seeing or hearing anything of the Yankees, thought it best to keep going until I did!

I rode steady on until I reached the Chickahominy, where I reported the Rebel troop movements that I had learned to the general. I said nothing of the band of men carrying Captain Hall's body back to camp.

Just got word—we have been ordered out tomorrow for battle. Pray for me, Mollie, and I for you.

Your friend,

$\mathcal{C}$.

Richmond, Virginia

June 1, 1862

Dear Emma,

The fighting is so close to us that we hear the sounds of cannons here in the city. I cannot help but wonder if you are there?

People have left Richmond by the hundreds. For weeks now, wagons heaped with trunks, boxes, and baskets have constantly rattled through the streets. It certainly does not breed confidence in the Confederacy to see the new congressmen and their families leaving town like scared rabbits. It doesn't help either to see the boxes and boxes of government documents marked for Columbia, South Carolina, stacked high outside of government offices.

Momma, Sissy, and I stay resolute. We will not leave our home. We went to St. Paul's the other day to sew ticking for beds for the wounded that are expected soon.

Last week, Mayor Mayo formed a Home Guard of boys sixteen to eighteen and men over forty-five. Charlie, almost fifteen, begs his mother to let him join the Confederates. She holds firm that he must be sixteen, but she told Charlie that if the Home Guard would let him enroll, she would permit it.

Charlie was ecstatic. He was sure he could pass for a sixteen-year-old. Sure enough, Emma, he is now an official member of the Richmond Home Guard. He is determined to protect our dear city, and marches around with a rusty musket gun that he doesn't know how to shoot.

What terrible news we hear! Losses are great on both sides. All this on the Sabbath, Emma. Oh I do pray you are well.

Your devoted friend,

Mollie

Richmond, Virginia

June 3, 1862

Dear Emma,

If only I had word of your safekeeping. Sissy waits for word of Lem. Sunday night the steady trail of wagons, carts, ambulances, and trains brought the wounded into Richmond. Monday, hospitals and private homes were once again filled with broken and wounded men. Momma took in three boys. Sissy and I walked around the city for two days trying to get word on Lem.

Yesterday we ran into Constance and Hetty. They promised their mother that they would search for their cousin, Reggie Hyde, who they had heard was wounded. We walked together down Main Street, going in and out of churches, hotels, and hospitals looking for Reggie and Lem.

Everywhere we looked we saw men desperately wounded and waiting for surgeons. Lying on bare boards, with only a knapsack under their heads, all were suffering horribly. Although we walked around the city all day, we did not find Reggie or Lem. Sissy and I fell exhausted onto our beds in our clothes last night. Sissy is being very brave. Constance, too.

When we checked the Ballard House Hotel, we didn't find our boys, but we did find newspaper reporters and plenty of curious citizens. Mrs. Greenhow and her five-year-old daughter had just arrived there. She is the famous Confederate spy who folks say sent the information to cause the Confederates to win the Battle of Manassas.

The Federals imprisoned Mrs. Greenhow with her daughter in the Capitol Prison in Washington, but President Lincoln's secretary of war just freed her. He permitted them to take a flag-of-truce boat to Richmond. I suppose he thinks them harmless now that they are among the Confederates. Strange. I would think a lady this clever could do just as much damage to the Federal cause here in Richmond as she did in Washington.

So many spies, here, Emma. Famous spies. And some not so famous spies, too!

Your friend,

Mollie

Richmond, Virginia

June 7, 1862

Dear Emma,

The fighting of this last week has brought such sorrow to Richmond. So many funerals. So much suffering. Sissy finally found Lem in a private hospital, bloody and suffering from a concussion. Thankfully, he still has all his arms and legs. Sissy brought him home to our house to nurse him. He is expected to make a full recovery.

There is much fighting. I will never forget the sounds so close to home. Constance and I went one day to the top of a building to see the battles. Your spy balloons hovered over the field. Even at night, we saw the bursts of the bombs and the flash of thousands of muskets. Every day, more and more ambulances arrive in Richmond with broken soldiers.

In the midst of it all, I received another delivery! Another book in a plain brown wrapper tied up with string. I slit open the binding of the book and found another set of coded notes. Using my code, I found this message: Roll of bandages. Same store.

I took a roll of bandages and unrolled it. At the center I placed the coded message, and then rolled it back up again.

The next morning, I went to Mr. Simpson's store. His wife was the proprietor that morning. I noticed she wore the peach pit pin. The clover design was pointing up so I knew not to speak with her about the message. "Do you have any more cloth for bandages, Mrs. Simpson?" I asked. "I can leave this roll with you, but I want to roll some more."

"I'm sorry, dear, we have no flannel or cotton right now," she replied. "I'll make sure this roll of bandages gets to where it can best help this war. Thank you, dear!"

I slipped out of the store. This time, Emma, I felt a bit more confident. As I turned down the street, guess who I ran into—Miss Van Lew. Only, it didn't look like her at all. She was dressed in buckskin leggings, a torn skirt, a cotton shirt, and an oversized floppy calico bonnet. She appeared not to notice anything, and sang little songs to herself. "Miss Van Lew!" I exclaimed. She walked right past me singing and talking to herself. I suppose this is the beginning of her Crazy Bet plan.

I walked behind her a bit just to study her outfit and ways. She kept humming and singing. Then suddenly, I realized I could understand her words. Over and over, she kept singing, "Pretty head. Pretty shoulders. A very good head on pretty shoulders." I had to keep from laughing as I realized she was sending me a message of congratulations for my first few missions.

As I turned around and walked away, I could see several of the women shaking their heads in disapproval at old Crazy Bet.

Your friend,

Mollie

Camp, near Richmond, Virginia

June 10, 1862

Dear Mollie,

I am well, but the Battle of Fair Oaks marks me forever! At the beginning of the battle on May 31st, General Philip Kearny assigned me to be his acting orderly. Mollie, I usually don't ride into battle. All day long, I rode wherever General Kearny rode and did whatever he asked me to do. You should see General Kearny in battle. The loss of his left arm from the Mexican War doesn't stop him one bit. Why, he'll catch his reins in his teeth and fight with his sword in his right hand.

The fighting was desperate. The rain-swollen Chickahominy River swamped the bridges and trapped the soldiers on the other side. General Kearny rode up and down the lines trying to encourage the men. He had sent several messages already to General McClellan at headquarters on the other side of the river about the need for reinforcements, but hours had gone by and none had arrived. Finally about two o'clock in the afternoon. General Kearny reined in his horse abruptly, took an envelope from his pocket, and wrote on the back of it: "In the name of God, bring your command to our relief, if you have to swim in order to get here—unless you come, we are lost." He handed it to me and said, "Go as fast as that horse can carry you to General Sumner, present this with my compliments, and return immediately to report to me."

I turned my horse and pushed him at top speed toward the river until he was nearly white with foam, then I plunged him into the Chickahominy River and swam him across. I met General Sumner about a hundred yards from the river. Engineers were working to strengthen the bridge and General McClelland ordered General Sumner to cross as soon as he could to come to our aid. The soldiers began to pour across the river on the planks and the entire division made it to the other side and started down the flooded road double time.

I swam my horse back across the river and raced to General Kearney in the thick of the fight. Riding up to him, I touched my hat and reported, "Just returned, sir. General Sumner, with his command, will be here immediately."

General Kearny swung around and shouted at the top of his voice, "Reinforcements! Reinforcements!" And swinging his hat in the air, he electrified the entire exhausted line.

Later that day, while I was riding with General Kearney, a Minnie ball whizzed by me and struck General Howard, knocking him from his horse and shattering his arm. Securing permission from General Kearney to attend to him, I jumped down from my horse, and hitched him nearby. I removed the clothing from General Howard's arm, gave him some water, poured some on the wound, and went to my saddlebags to get some bandages. Just then old Reb, the horse I took from the enemy during my second spying mission as Bridget, turned on me and bit me hard, tearing part of the flesh from my arm. Searing pain shot through my arm, but I made a sling and continued to help General Howard.

Later, after the battle, General Howard's arm was amputated above the elbow. General Kearney stayed with him the entire time. There are so many men who have died and many more who are wounded. The surgeons couldn't care for them all. We spent most of our days after the battle pouring cool water on the wounds while they waited for the surgeons to tend to them.

There is a tree that stands at Fair Oaks. It is an immense oak tree called the Hospital Tree where under its shade, the wounded rested. I cannot bear to write about what I saw there that day. Thousands fell during those battles. Thousands more are maimed and wounded. There is so much death and destruction—quite enough to make angels weep.

The day after the battle, General Kearney presented me with a Confederate officer's sword, which had been found on the battlefield. He said it was in appreciation for the great bravery I showed on the field as his orderly that day. In return, I gave him Reb, but warned him he should be kept away from any valiant officers he valued!

My arm hurts something awful, Mollie, but it will not need to be amputated. Don't worry, I can still write. I am more discouraged of heart, though, as I reflect upon all I have seen during the Battle of Fair Oaks.

Your friend,

$\mathcal{C}$.

Richmond, Virginia

June 15, 1862

Dear Emma,

Charlie came by today bursting with news. General Jeb Stuart rode into town to meet with General Robert E. Lee. Emma, it isn't good news for the Federals. Here's what happened. General Stuart and twelve hundred cavalrymen rode in a large circle around General McClelland's forces over the last four days to spy out how many men you have, how strong the forces are, and what positions you are in. He rode into town jauntily today with all his cavalry and more than a hundred Yankee prisoners, some runaway slaves, and some horses and mules behind him.

Richmond rejoices at this news! It was a bold move on the part of General Stuart. Sissy is ecstatic as Lem was one of those cavalrymen. I am sure General Lee will use this to his advantage. Please be careful.

Your friend,

Mollie

Richmond, Virginia

June 16, 1862

Dear Emma,

Another mission today! As usual, I carved from the spine of the book the coded messages—one for another's eyes, one for mine. This time the message said: Meet me. Libby.

I couldn't tell from Miss Van Lew's message whether I was supposed to bring the coded message with me or not. I took a thick ribbon and wrapped it over the message several times and then tied it up in my hair. I walked quickly to the bench near Libby Prison and waited for Miss Van Lew. Crazy Bet showed up carrying a platter wrapped in a towel and a basket of books over her arm.

"Miss Van Lew," I said, "I thought we weren't going to be seen together again."

"Yes, I know, but much is happening now with General McClelland and his troops ready to enter Richmond. Time is of the essence, and I had to take this chance. New Federal prisoners arrived yesterday. I must get into the prison, and I need your help. More and more each day I arouse suspicion. I thought today a distraction in the way of a lovely young Rebel girl accompanying me might be nice."

"What is in the platter?"

"Nothing secretive this time," she replied. I knew Miss Van Lew had a platter with a false bottom that concealed letters and other information. "Just a wonderful custard. But I need a splendid conversationalist to keep them busy so that I can have as much time as possible inside the prison."

I thought for a few moments and then agreed to do it. "But what about the book you sent me . . . and its message inside."

"Yes. You can take that to Mrs. Simpson at the store. Later. Do you think you can give me at least twenty minutes inside?"

"Miss Van Lew, I think it will take them twenty minutes just to stop looking at you. You do look a sight!" Again we laughed, as she looked down at her buckskin leggings, her calico skirt, her tattered shirt, and her floppy bonnet.

"Why thank you, Miss Mollie! I get so many compliments on my new outfit."

We laughed again. "I bet you do!"

"The crazier they think I am," she explained, "the more they leave me alone."

My heart was pounding when we got inside. The warden nudged another officer when Miss Van Lew walked up to him. I heard him whisper to the officer, "Crazy Bet's here again."

"Kind sir, I came to collect my books. Miss Turner here will help me carry them back to my home. She is kind to me, although her mother doesn't like her associating with me much any more." Then Miss Van Lew lowered her voice and whispered, "She thinks I'm crazy."

"I remember this young girl from your earlier trips to Libby, Miss Van Lew. She used to help you then—carry the books, I mean."

"Yes, and I prevailed on her one more time because of my heavy load. She is a dear. Nurses at Robertson Hospital many days."

At the sound of the beloved Confederate hospital run by Captain Sally Tompkins, the men seemed to relax. When Miss Van Lew explained the custard was for them to eat, they seemed more than willing to let her in the prison to visit the men. When she was gone, I offered to serve the warden and his officer some custard. They gathered plates, and I slowly dished out the sweet dessert.

"Do you know Captain Tompkins?" I asked.

"No, no, we don't. But there isn't a wounded soldier who doesn't want to be assigned to her hospital," they responded. "Nearly all her charges live to see another battle."

"She is a remarkable woman," I continued, "and runs the hospital as well as any general."

As the men settled back in their chairs and began to enjoy their custard, I told them story after story of Captain Tompkins and Robertson Hospital. "The ladies of Richmond say it is their favorite hospital for volunteering. I don't know how much the men like it though. One day, I overheard a young boy respond to one of the volunteers asked to wash his face, 'Why ma'am, of course you can, but you'd be the fourteenth lady today to scrub it clean.'"

The men laughed, and I began to relax. I continued on with stories about Captain Sally, sewing at St. Paul's, Sissy's trips to follow Lem's regiment, and the number of wounded we have nursed in our home. By the time Miss Van Lew returned, they were thoroughly convinced of my Confederate sympathies.

I hoped it served to allay some suspicion about Miss Van Lew. But when she came back through again with the prison official, she was acting as crazy as ever. I leaned over to the warden and whispered, "We must do what we can for the less fortunate of the Richmond ladies, don't you agree? This war has affected her so." He nodded knowingly, and we slipped quickly out of the prison.

We walked quickly up the hill to Grace Street and the Van Lew mansion. Momma told me that Confederate General Johnson had been wounded at the Battle of Fair Oaks and was recuperating at a friend's house on Grace Street. Miss Van Lew confirmed it. Imagine that! Confederate generals and Federal spies on the same street!

I carried the platter into her house, and we both relaxed at the table with a cup of contraband tea her Federal contacts had given her. I mimicked Crazy Bet to her, and she laughed at me. "I hope that will throw them off for a while. Hopefully, it won't be much longer before General McClelland arrives and this is a Federal city again. Mother has made up a special guest room for the general. With what I learned today, it shouldn't be long. Now, Mollie, I want to add something to the message you already have. Would you be so kind as to wait while I encode the message?"

When she returned, I unwound my hair and ribbon, added the second message, and then wound it all up again. Miss Van Lew studied me solemnly the entire time. When it was time to leave, she said, "Mollie, you certainly do have a good head on those pretty shoulders of yours." She gave me a hug and said, "From now on, when you see Crazy Bet, pay attention to what she sings. You never know what might be hidden in her little ditties." What a day!

Your friend,

Mollie

Vicinity of Fair Oaks

June 27, 1862

Dear Mollie,

I needed to give my arm time to heal, so I asked for a week's leave to visit the hospitals in Williamsburg and Yorktown. In Williamsburg, I attended meetings in the evening held by a minister from the Christian Commission for the Benefit of Wounded Soldiers. In several powerful sermons, the minister described the tender mercies of the Father and the love of the Son, Jesus. He preached Christ with such simplicity that many were moved to tears.

From Yorktown, I went down to White House Landing, a quiet little country village. After spending a day there, I was tired of idleness and ready to return to Fair Oaks. I boarded a train and whom should I see but the old peddler who spied on General McClelland for the Confederacy. Apparently, he was sick or wounded because two men carried him from the train on a stretcher. At the station, he was trying to get the attention of people passing by—asking for help. I spotted the Federal Provost Marshal and quickly told him everything I knew about this Rebel spy. I watched as he approached the peddler. I'm sure he got all the attention he deserved!

I'm glad I had a time of refreshment for no sooner did I return than there was another battle—this time at Gaines Mill. The surgeons and nurses could not keep up with all the wounded. Thank goodness the Christian Commission is here. Not only do they bring the good news of the Gospel, but they work hour after hour with the surgeons. They dress wounds, carry water to the thirsty, and speak words of comfort to the dying. If a man is dying, they make sure he knows there is the free gift of salvation given through Jesus Christ. These men from the Christian Commission are a great encouragement to us during this campaign.

Your tired friend,

C.

Richmond, Virginia

July 2, 1862

Dear Emma,

Wagon upon wagon brings more wounded and dead to the city. It has been a nightmare. Charlie brings the papers over each day so Sissy can confirm that Lem is not listed as a casualty. She is desperate for word from him. Momma and I have been giving as much time as we can to nurse the wounded. There is no room left in the hospitals, so stores and homes are makeshift hospitals. Sissy and our boarders care for two soldiers in our home, while Momma and I work at Robertson Hospital.

Hundreds and hundreds of Yankee prisoners march to the prisons. I scan each of their faces to make sure yours is not among them.

I've had no messages lately, which is just as good. Mr. Simpson's store is filled with wounded Confederates. Not a good time to take a message to him to pass on to the Federals.

Are you wounded, Emma? Please send word as soon as possible.

Your worried friend,

Mollie

Camp near Harrison's Landing

July 3, 1862

Dear Mollie,

I received my orders to ride to several hospitals to tell the surgeons, nurses, and those wounded who are able to walk to leave as quickly as possible. Ambulances couldn't reach them in time. The Union army was retreating toward the James River, and they would fall into the hands of the Confederates if they remained much longer. I've learned that one of the brave surgeon's assistants refused to leave the helpless men. He was taken prisoner and brought to Richmond. His name is Jerome Robbins of the Second Michigan Regiment. If you do go to Libby Prison again, please find out if he is there.

I rode back as fast as possible through the hail of Minnie balls falling around me. At one point, I saw a large number of soldiers. They wore the uniform of the Federals and I was much relieved. I urged my horse on faster and when I came within a hundred yards of them, a soldier waved his hand to direct me another way. I realized they were prisoners guarded by a band of Rebels, and hightailed it out of there. Another volley of Minnie balls showered down in my path, but none touched me. Riding between two lines with a blaze of musketry and artillery, I knew that nothing but the power of the Almighty could have shielded me from such a storm of shot and shell and brought me through unscathed. It was for me as much of a miracle as that of Shadrach, Meshach, and Abednego coming forth from the fiery furnace without even the smell of fire upon them.

Your friend,

Ꞡ.

Richmond, Virginia

July 12, 1862

Dear Emma,

Another book and another message. This time when I unscrambled the message, it read: Basket of eggs.

We have no chickens. Eggs have been scarce for months. The only place I have seen a basket of eggs was at Miss Van Lew's home. Surely she did not mean for me to come to her house. She is Crazy Bet now, wandering around the prisons filled with Federal soldiers, singing her little ditties to herself, and scooping up lots of information while hospital and prison wardens laugh at her. Harmless old Bet. Crazy old Bet. Crazy like a fox, I say!

It was a warm day, so I sat outside on the veranda. Charlie came by just to let me know Richmond is safe under his watchful eye. He put his rusty musket in the corner and spread the newspapers out on the table. Of course, the papers say the Confederacy is winning, but I imagine the Washington papers say the Union is winning.

While we were sitting outside, a man pulled up in his hack. "Whoa!" he said to the horses and then hopped out. "Good day, Miss Mollie."

Having no idea who he was, I said, "Good day, sir."

Then I noticed his peach pit pin. Wanting to warn him, I said, "This is Charlie. He is protecting our home front, but he really wishes he could be fighting for the Confederacy."

"Why, hello, young Charlie. Miss Mollie, Mrs. Simpson felt so badly about that jar of pickled peaches she sold to you that turned out to be rotten. She would like you to accept this basket of fresh eggs with her apologies."

"Why that is quite kind of you. Please tell Mrs. Simpson that this basket of eggs is most appreciated."

I took the basket inside, and told Charlie I would be back in a moment with a cool drink for him. Once inside, I began to lift the eggs out of the basket and found one was as light as a feather. It must be hollow. I held it up to the light and saw a message inside. I took it to my room and then returned to the veranda with a glass filled with Confederate lemonade for Charlie. Oh, for another lemon like Lem brought to us last month from the cavalry raid!

As soon as Charlie left, I broke open the egg. How clever of Miss Van Lew! Two small pieces of paper rolled up tight had been inserted through a narrow hole in the top of the egg. One was the coded message. I spread the other paper out next to my cipher and unscrambled the message: Bandages. Store.

I immediately knew what to do. I ripped part of the sheet from my bed and began to tear the cloth into strips. I rolled each one up into a bandage, but there was one that was tighter than the others to make sure the message inside did not show or slip out. I marked that bandage with a peach pit from the pickled peaches. I knew Mrs. Simpson would understand.

I walked down to the store with my basket of bandages. Mrs. Simpson moved around tending to the wounded with such tenderness, I realized that although her loyalties are with the North, her mother's heart is with these boys. I admired her for a few moments before I got her attention. "More bandages, ma'am. Made them special for you." She nodded knowingly and took the basket full of bandages to the back of the store. I was sure she would find the single most important bandage in the basket.

A boy lifted his head and whispered, "Water." I found a ladle and scooped up some water from the bucket and poured in gently into his mouth. His eyes signaled his appreciation as he slipped back into unconsciousness. Oh, Emma, when will this cruel war be over?

I simply must hear that you are safe. All this fighting around Richmond has kept even the private couriers from getting our letters to each other. I hope you have heard from me, and that I will hear from you soon.

Your friend,

Mollie

Richmond, Virginia

August 3, 1862

Dear Emma,

Sissy has decided to run the blockade, and I'm going with her. Sissy has it fixed in her head that she must make Lem a new uniform of Confederate gray wool with shining gold buttons. Lem has been promoted again, and Sissy insists he must have a uniform befitting his position. We all thought she was teasing at first, but the more Sissy turned the idea over in her head, the more determined she became. Thread, needles, Confederate gray wool, buttons, gold lace. All these are contraband articles and the only way to get them is to run the blockade, purchase them in the land of the Federals, and then smuggle them back across the line.

At first, Momma objected, but then she has objected to every one of Sissy's adventures to see Lem. Once it was clear Sissy was going to run the blockade, Momma encouraged me to go with her. She thinks I can keep Sissy from being arrested.

Momma has Confederate scrip for us to use until we get to the Federal line and gold to use once we are inside Federal territory. Momma sewed some false pockets inside our petticoats for hiding the gold. It will weigh us down, but it is the only medium of exchange for purchasing contraband goods. I think Momma would like us to get a few items for her, too. She hasn't said anything yet, but I see the gleam in her eye when she hears Sissy talk about new needles and thread.

We will find Great-Auntie once we get to Baltimore, Momma and I are both worried about Great-Auntie. We haven't heard from her in so long. Lem will try to arrange a pass for us at least to the Federal line. Lem thinks we should try to go north by going west first to Culpeper and then north through Point of Rocks, across to Maryland, and then on to Baltimore. The direct route north from Richmond is in the path of the battles and far too dangerous.

I have sent a coded message to Miss Van Lew to let her know my plans and that I won't be available to pass on messages for a while. I took the message to Mrs. Simpson, and she agreed to pass it on.

I desperately want to be with Great-Auntie. I've missed her so much. That alone is worth the risk.

Your adventurous friend,

Mollie

Richmond, Virginia

August 15, 1862

Dear Emma,

We leave tomorrow. Early this morning, I received a visit from Mr. Simpson. He brought a jar of pickled peaches for Momma and a book for me. I took the book to my room and found another coded message in the spine. But there was no message inside in our special code. I looked all over the book but could find no other hidden message. I flipped through the pages but they were unmarked. Then I saw the title of the book: *The History of Baltimore.* Is this message supposed to go to Baltimore? Who gets it? Where do I take it?

We had much to do, but I slipped away and walked to Mr. and Mrs. Simpson's store. Mrs. Simpson greeted me and guided me to the back storeroom. Her peach pit pin indicated it was okay to speak to her. She spoke in hushed tones. "Mollie, Betty needs your help. She has information she must get to a certain general. She tried to take it herself and start it out on the relay stations, but she is being very carefully watched right now.

"She went out early last evening to bring the message to our store, and a man passed by her and said, 'Going North tonight?' She thought that was odd, so she started muttering to herself in her best Crazy Bet manner. The man passed by her again and said, 'Going North tonight?' but again Betty just walked on. It's a good thing she did, too. It turns out this was a Confederate officer in civilian clothes trying to trap her. She must be extremely careful now. She has vital information that must get to the right person across the lines but she fears her normal relay stations are being watched, too."

"I have the message, but I don't know who is to get it," I explained. "Miss Van Lew didn't say anything to me about who is supposed to get the message or how I will get it to him."

"She'll let you know somehow, Mollie. Now leave quickly before any of the customers become suspicious. Godspeed, Mollie."

When I left the store, guess who I saw walking around in circles, singing little songs. That's right—Crazy Bet. As I walked toward home, she walked by me, singing:

> *Adam was first, then came Eve*
> *R-S or was it T-U-V?*
> *Sing at night; sing in the morning,*
> *Dance all day, but noon is best.*
> *Monday, Tuesday, Wednesday pie,*
> *Thursday, Friday, Saturday cry.*
> *Check the clock!*
> *Not much time!*

That was all, Emma—just that crazy rhyme. How am I supposed to figure out who gets this message in Baltimore and when? All the way home, I turned the rhyme over and over in my head. Nothing makes any sense. How can Miss Van Lew trust me with such an important message when I can't understand her clues?

Confused, I remain your faithful friend,

Mollie

Culpeper, Virginia

August 16, 1862

Dear Emma,

    I'll have to bundle these letter together for a while until I'm in Federal land. Then I'll post them to you directly through the Federal mail with United States stamps. Momma helped me make a false bottom to our trunk. I am sure even the most diligent search will not reveal it. I will keep these letters in there until I can mail them to you.

    We took the train from Richmond, and arrived at Culpeper this afternoon near Lem's unit. We stayed at a boardinghouse and shared a room with two other ladies. They also planned to run the blockade, and had hired a wagon and driver. They had room for two more passengers and a couple of trunks. Sissy wanted to confer with Lem, but I knew a good deal when I saw it.

    We had a nice supper and fell asleep easily, assured that we would soon be on our way.

Your friend, the blockade runner,

Mollie

Somewhere in Virginia

August 17, 1862

Dear Emma,

Sissy was not at all assured when we saw our transportation. The wagon turned out to be an old cart with wide planks spread side by side across the axles with two chairs perched precariously in a large quantity of straw on the makeshift floor. When the two other ladies saw this royal carriage, they decided we were welcome to it and would wait until something suitable was available. Sissy and I both agreed that from what we could see, that could be a very long wait. Anything suitable had been confiscated for use by the army long ago.

We pushed our two small trunks up in the cart and then climbed up and tried to steady ourselves on the chairs. Giving up, we settled down in the straw on the boards. Our rugged driver snapped the reins and we were off. We stopped tonight at a ramshackle farmhouse. The farmer's wife was kind enough to us, though, and we slept on straw mattresses on the floor.

My body aches from the swaying of the wagon over the ruts in the road. I am dreaming of Great-Auntie's featherbed.

Your bone-weary friend,

Mollie

Top of the Blue Ridge Mountains

August 19, 1862

Dear Emma,

After another long day of travel in our wagon, our driver stopped at a small cottage and asked about lodging for the night. Sissy and I, weary from our travels, were more than ready to fall asleep, but the mountain woman gave us such a delightful supper of fresh eggs, milk, cream, bread, and apple butter that we found ourselves renewed. We stayed up and talked with the dear woman for many hours. She was hungry for news of the war.

This morning, her husband—a scruffy mountain man—grumbled that we might want to see something. We followed him up a path. When he stopped, we looked out where he was staring and gasped. The early morning sun broke through a beautiful mist rising on the mountains. We could see miles and miles of beautiful country—our beautiful Virginia—unstained by human blood, untouched by weapons of war. We were silent for quite some time, but I know both Sissy and I were thinking of happier times.

It was difficult to leave such a beautiful place. We insisted they take our money even though they didn't want to.

After all, we told them, a good night's sleep after days of riding in that wagon was priceless!

Sissy gave me a look as she stepped up again into our special carriage. I think even she was beginning to wonder if a new uniform was worth all this agony.

After another day in the wagon, we reached Berryville and yet another boardinghouse. We went to bed early. Tomorrow will find us inside Federal lines. Sissy and I quietly rehearsed our story as we lay in bed.

If anyone asks, we are worried sick about our great-auntie who means so much to us. We have to check on her. If asked our purpose for traveling without a pass from the War Department, we will explain that our great-uncle would have gotten us a pass, but as a surgeon for the wounded Union troops, he could not be located—another reason we felt such urgency to see about our precious auntie. If they checked on us, they would surely verify that he was a Federal officer, just like them. Sissy wanted to tell them she was the proud wife of a Confederate officer, but I strongly urged her to remember that for this trip and for this moment, we are just two sisters who desperately want to make sure their great-aunt is all right.

Tomorrow we cross the line.

Your daring friend,

Mollie

Berlin, Maryland

August 20, 1862

Dear Emma,

Our driver brought us to the Potomac River and told us we were on our own now. A boat crowded with Federal soldiers hugged the shore of Virginia. It was easy enough to secure passage on the boat, but whether we would be a prisoner once on the Maryland shore was yet unknown. Sissy shook with fear, and I squeezed her hand. That kept one hand busy, but the other one twisted her curls over and over. If Sissy were a spy, she should never keep secret messages hidden in her hair for they would surely fall out with all her twisting.

I thought about my secret message and the letters to you. Last night, after Sissy fell asleep, I removed them from the false bottom in the trunk and sewed them up in my petticoat. I have heard that everyone, including women, are searched, but I thought them safer there than in the trunk, which we knew for certain would be searched.

When we got to the other side in Maryland (clearly inside Federal lines), a Federal captain told us to wait. Sissy continued to shake, and I tried to have enough confidence for both of us. The Federals detained several others from the boat as well. I gazed at each of them. A girl, about nine years old, clung to her mother. An older man, with a long beard, buried himself in his newspaper. A young man tapped his foot as his eyes darted back and forth. He seemed to me to have the most to lose in these interviews. Why would a man who could be fighting for either side be standing there in civilian clothes wanting to cross without a pass? Could he be a spy, too?

The captain asked each of us to declare who we were and what our purpose was in Federal lands. I observed everything and took mental notes. The mother and child passed with flying colors. It seemed that the captain knew the woman's husband, a Federal soldier. The woman and her daughter had been caught behind Rebel lines visiting family as the battle lines shifted. They were not searched, although their trunk was. Then the captain interviewed the old man. He lived in Maryland, but had taken his sick wife back to visit her daughter at her home in Virginia before the war started. There she had died, and he now needed to come back home. He had proof of his identification and papers showing he owned a home in Maryland. He, too, quickly passed on through without even having his trunk searched.

Then the captain turned to the nervous young man. The captain spent twice as much time interviewing him. He said he was studying medicine in Baltimore. His sister had been visiting him there and he had seen her back home. Now he was returning to continue his studies. I could tell the captain did not believe him. Both his person and his trunk were searched, and he was detained for a further interview with the marshal.

Now it was our turn. Sissy took a deep breath. She sat on her hands to keep from twisting her hair. She told me later that she kept the image of the brand new uniform in mind the whole time to give her enough strength to stop shaking. She did not want to give us away.

Although Sissy was older, the captain directed most of the questions to me. "Young lady, where do you live?"

"Richmond . . . with our momma."

His eyes narrowed, "And your father?"

"He died two years ago, and now it is just Momma, Sissy, and me."

"No brothers?"

I could tell he wanted to know where our fighting sympathies fell so I answered this way: "No brothers, no male cousins, no father. It is just us girls helping Momma with her boarders."

That seemed to satisfy him on that score. "Where are you traveling?"

Bless Sissy, this is where her flair for the dramatic became our saving grace. "Dear Captain, dear Captain, you must help us!" Sissy exclaimed. "We are desperately worried about Great-Auntie. She lives in Baltimore and we have had no word from her in months. Momma is beside herself and sent us to face whatever danger we must to find out whether Great-Auntie is well. She and Great-Uncle Chester are all we have left of Daddy. We must make sure she is safe." Tears poured down Sissy's face, and I dabbed at her eyes with my handkerchief.

"Sir," I continued anticipating his next question, "our great-uncle Chester is a Union officer. He was a doctor in Washington before the war and offered his services to the Union as a surgeon at the beginning of the war. With so many battles and so many wounded, we have no idea where he is now. But you can check. In fact, you might be able to put us in touch with him. That would be very much appreciated. We would love to see him too, but it is Great-Auntie Belle we are most concerned about. She is alone in Baltimore. Great-Uncle Chester moved her there months ago when Washington became an army camp."

He seemed convinced and left us alone. Sissy let out a big sigh, and I put my arm around her and squeezed her shoulder. I lowered my voice and whispered, "You were marvelous!" Sissy sat up a bit straighter, quite proud of her performance.

After an hour, the captain returned with word that the marshal would check out our story, but it would take time. We would not be able to leave until tomorrow morning at the earliest. The captain directed us to a boardinghouse where we spent a lovely evening with a nice couple.

They seemed to know all about crossing the line. They said that most folks are turned back. He told us they have women search the women so that they can examine each article of clothing to see if anything is being smuggled one way or the other. Sissy and I looked at each other, and I saw the fear in her eyes. She knew that we carried only gold for this part of the journey; but I could tell she was thinking about our return trip. She did not know about my letters to you or my secret message. Of course, I have not written any names or addresses on envelopes. I have only kept my letters directed to *Emma*. Later, I will address the envelopes when I can send these safely.

After dinner, a man knocked on the door and delivered our two small trunks to us. Our host took them to our room and when we retired for the night, we examined them. Our clothes were in disarray, but it was clear they had not discovered the false bottom in my trunk. Momma should be proud—she is as good a spy as you and me!

I don't think our sleep will be sweet tonight, but we have made it this far and for that, we are thankful. Good night, dear Federal friend. I sleep in your territory tonight as you have slept in mine near Richmond. Imagine how close we must have been during the Seven Days Battles and yet I could only know your presence by the flame and smoke of rifles and cannons.

Your friend,

Mollie

Berlin, Maryland

August 21, 1862

Dear Emma,

We awoke to strong rapping on the door this morning. Having slept in our clothes, we were downstairs in a flash. The captain said, "The marshal has granted you permission to go. The train to Baltimore leaves in fifteen minutes." I asked if he had passes for us to Baltimore, and he explained that we had made it through this checkpoint, but it would be up to other Federal officers to pass us through their checkpoints.

We were very happy as the train rolled out of the station until we realized that the marshal's deputy was sitting a few seats behind us. Was he following us? He seemed to be keeping us under close observation. Sissy read a Federal newspaper, and I read *The History of Baltimore*. Both of us looked over our paper or book to see him looking over his newspaper watching us. Hadn't they bought our story back at Berlin?

Although we were anxious, the train chugged along, and we were hopeful we would get to Baltimore without any more trouble. Our hopes were dashed when a man got on at one of the stops, conferred with the deputy, and then glanced our way. We continued to act as if we were unconcerned, but both our hearts were pounding.

At the next stop, the marshal's deputy and the other man walked up to us, showed us their badges, and asked us to leave the train. They had us identify our trunks, and then they removed them from the train. We stood on the platform watching our train to Baltimore chug out of the station. Sissy and I looked at each other and didn't say a word. We each knew what the other was thinking. Had we come this close only to be sent back home or worse—imprisoned?

The men escorted us to a small office in the train station. There we watched as they searched our trunks again. They patted the sides and tried to lift the bottom of Sissy's trunk. I held my breath as they searched my trunk and when they patted the bottom. I was glad my letters were safely sewn into the lining of my petticoat. They found nothing.

A woman deputy searched our persons. She patted down Sissy's clothes and found our gold. Sissy said, "Momma gave it to us because Confederate notes certainly would not buy us train tickets to Baltimore." She seemed satisfied and let us keep the gold. If it had been confiscated, we would really have been in trouble.

I held my breath. She patted down my skirts but somehow missed the letters. But then she saw my book that I held in my arms the entire time. I took in a quick breath. This could be the end. Last night, concerned about the coded message, I had returned it to its original hiding place in the spine of the book. Even though it was a message for the Federals, I couldn't prove it because it was in code. If discovered, they might think I was spying for the Confederacy. I wouldn't want to have Miss Van

Lew vouch for me and compromise her network of secret spies. I prayed that what had worked time and time again to get messages in and out of Libby Prison would work once more now. I began to prattle on about the book and how I was learning so much about Baltimore and its history and that my Great-Auntie would be so proud and that she always wanted me to know more about Northern things. The searcher flipped through the book, turned it upside down, and shook it. Satisfied, she returned it to me, and I clutched it all the tighter, saying a prayer of thanks.

Once again we had to tell our story, and once again, Sissy performed remarkably well. You would have thought Great-Auntie Belle was on her deathbed, and we were the only ones in the universe who could save her.

Finally, the deputy and the new marshal waved us on. We waited four hours on the train platform for the next train to Baltimore. It was only when we boarded the train that we both broke down. Both of us shook so hard we thought we might throw the train off its tracks. All the way to Baltimore, Sissy twisted her hair, but I said not one word. I could certainly forgive her nervous habit this time!

Emma, how do you do this every day? It is so nerve-racking! I have even more respect than ever for what you have done with your life.

Your exhausted friend,

Mollie

Baltimore, Maryland

August 22, 1862

Dear Emma,

Oh the joy we felt when we hugged Great-Auntie. We could not wait to get to her home. We stayed up until three o'clock in the morning talking and laughing. Great-Auntie exclaimed over and over, "My adventurous girls!" She didn't even seem to mind that Sissy's purpose in running the blockade was to secure cloth, thread, and buttons for a Confederate uniform. Great-Auntie is so pleased with Sissy's courage that she said she will do everything she can to help her get those contraband goods.

I went to sleep happy and tired, but with other things on my mind as well. Now that we were safe in Baltimore, I had to deliver the message to Miss Van Lew's contact. On the train, I went over and over again the rhyme Miss Van Lew sang:

Adam was first, then came Eve
R-S or was it T-U-V?
Sing at night; sing in the morning,
Dance all day, but noon is best.
Monday, Tuesday, Wednesday pie,

Thursday, Friday, Saturday cry.
Check the clock!
Not much time!

All I could tell for sure was that there wasn't much time. I had to be swift in solving this riddle or else the information would be too late to be of any use to the Federal government.

Surely in these crazy words is the name of the person to get the message, as well as the place to meet him or her. But even if I figure out who and where, how will I know when? She lists every day but Sunday in the rhyme.

Oh, I wish Miss Van Lew had not been so mysterious. Why didn't she just sing her crazy little song with real words, real clues? I puzzled all day about it but had no ideas. Another day passes that the message stays in the spine of my book, while I worry I am too late.

Your confused friend,

Mollie

Baltimore, Maryland

August 23, 1862

Dear Emma,

Today I did not think about messages, secret codes, or the war. Today I shopped! Do you know how long it has been since I have been in a store with hats and clothes and ribbons and lace? Great-Auntie took Sissy and I to the shops on Charles Street, and we were like two kids in a candy store. We touched the beautiful silk dresses. We tried on hat after hat. I had to purchase one for myself even though Sissy told me I would never be able to smuggle such a large item back through enemy lines. The shopkeeper said these hats are all the rage in Paris now.

I suppose I wanted something frivolous to remember this extraordinary journey by and to share with Momma. I knew we girls would get good use out of this hat if I could just get it back to Richmond. Besides, it would fold, so perhaps smuggling it through was not out of the question. As Great-Auntie said, what was the worst that could happen? It would be confiscated, and I would lose the money I had spent on it. That was a small enough risk to me. I may have a good head on my shoulders, but sometimes this good head likes to look pretty!

At the end of the day, we stopped for a pastry and some tea at a bakery shop. It was a delicious day, all around. Treats and sweets. It was a day for girlish fun in girlish ways and something we have missed for so long in this interminable war.

Your friend,

Mollie

Baltimore, Maryland

August 24, 1862

Dear Emma,

   After our shopping, we came back to Great-Auntie's home and laughed until we cried. Sissy and I both are worn out with the war and Great-Auntie seemed to know that. She let us both pile into her featherbed with her that night and snuggle close. We slept like babies.

   This morning, Great-Auntie asked if Sissy and I would go back down to the bakery on Charles Street. In all the excitement, she had forgotten to bring home her box of sweet breads she purchased yesterday for our breakfast. Sissy and I jumped at the chance to get out again with such freedom. Baltimore is not at all like Richmond. Shops here are for shopping, not makeshift hospitals. There is a sense of regular life going on with people scurrying along to take care of their errands. People greet each other with hellos and good-days and tips of their hats. It reminds us of Richmond before the war.

   Sissy and I skipped along the streets and giggled like little girls. When we got to the bakery, the baker asked us to wait a moment because he had to pull his pies out of the oven. They smelled heavenly. Sissy and I wondered if we could spare some of our precious money to purchase a pie. Even Sissy's hoard of sugar had been gone for months now, so the smells in the bakery astounded us. We licked our lips thinking about the sweet juices of a berry pie.

"Sorry to keep you so long, ladies," the baker said, "but with the rations, I can only bake pies on Mondays, Tuesdays, and Wednesdays. What can I get for you?"

It's a good thing Sissy conducted the business because I was astonished. The baker gave me the first clue. When we left, the clock above his shop began to chime. That's it! This is the spot I am to meet the person for the message. Maybe it is the baker himself, like Mr. and Mrs. Simpson. I told Sissy to wait just a minute, and I ran back inside. Boldly, I asked him, "Do you like pickled peaches?" He look surprised, said, "Never had them," and returned to his baking.

I puzzled about it all the way home to Great-Auntie's. Great-Auntie was thrilled with our surprise pie and said we should slice it very thin so that it would last all week. After breakfast, she announced she was taking us to a tailor's shop—a special tailor's shop. She said she would forget her Yankee sensibilities for the day to assist Sissy in her venture.

When we arrived, we learned that this tailor kept materials for Confederate uniforms hidden in his back room. The tailor whispered, "I have to be very careful. The Yankees watch me. Come with me. I have several pieces of excellent Confederate cloth. Who is this for?"

Sissy said, "Kind sir, my husband is a captain and has just been promoted again. He must look the part of such a grand officer."

The tailor said, "Indeed! How do you plan to carry this cloth back across the lines?"

Great-Auntie answered that we are waiting to obtain a pass from the War Department and sail on the flag-of-truce boat to Richmond.

He replied, "Then why don't you wear that uniform cloth right in front of those Yankee patrols!" Seeing the surprise on our faces, he explained, "I'll cut the cloth into proper lengths for you to make the uniform. Then I'll stitch those panels for you and your sister to wear home under your birdcage skirts."

Sissy and I looked at each other and grinned. "Just like Hetty!" we exclaimed together.

He seemed so pleased with himself, but then his face darkened. "Oh dear," he mumbled, "these buttons are another matter. They clearly state they are Confederate army. "Hmmm . . ." he said, "I shall cover them with wadding and cloth for you to button the panels like petticoats to your skirts!"

That problem solved, Sissy presented him with another. Sissy asked for enough plaid flannel to make Lem a new shirt. "Hmmm—" he said again. Our tailor tapped his temple as if he were willing an idea to jump out of his head. Then suddenly his face brightened. "Shawls! I'll make you two plaid shawls from enough material to cut into shirts when you return."

I asked, "Isn't it a bit warm for shawls?"

"Yes," he replied, "but along the water, it will be cool. You will have need of them."

Great-Auntie chimed in, "I plan to accompany them by the flag-of-truce boat, so make a shawl for me as well." We all laughed and then shushed each other—three ladies and their tailor in a great conspiracy for getting material back to the South.

"Now, needles and thread, and gold lace for the uniform," reminded Sissy. The tailor had ideas for that as well as he studied Great-Auntie's rather large purse. He asked if she could leave it with him. When she picked it up, the bottom would have new lining with the lace and needles and thread all folded smooth and sewn up inside.

A marvelous day! You see, Emma, we too have a disguise! We are three ladies who will be wearing a Confederate uniform in front of everyone—but no one will know. Now if only I could have as much success with my message.

Your friend,

Mollie

Washington, D.C.

August 26, 1862

Dear Mollie,

We were close to Richmond. Our men were discouraged after much fighting to then turn away. Our regiment marched to Newport News and then on to Aquia Creek. We were not there long before we were off to support General Pope's army in the Shenandoah Valley. I wished I could have been with them, but I was needed for other secret missions. My job as Regimental Postmaster gives me great freedom and cover for these missions.

I have now had four assignments behind enemy lines, but this was my most memorable one. General Heintzelman wanted me to go behind enemy lines and get information about the enemy's troops. This time, I disguised myself as a female slave. Once I crossed the Rebel lines, I joined a group of nine slaves who serve the needs of the Rebel army. An officer ordered me to headquarters to prepare his meal.

Again, I was surprised how openly the Rebels speak about their troops and their plans. The Federals keep maneuvers and locations of troops a secret from the soldiers. But here, all you have to do is be in the right place, listen, and remember what you hear.

It didn't take long for me to hear the officers discussing their plans for the next day. At first they spoke in low tones, but then they became excited and, forgetting us slaves, spoke freely. They even mentioned the number of reinforcements and when they would arrive.

The next morning, I cooked breakfast with the other slaves. As I moved a campstool that stood in my way, papers fell from the pockets of a coat laid over the stool. I quickly grabbed them and stuffed them into my own pockets, hidden in the dress I wore. I had to leave immediately before someone noticed the documents were missing.

I crept toward the picket line that was nearest to the Federals. I made my way to an old house and hid myself in the cellar. Within moments, the Federals and the Rebels began firing at each other. Cannonballs and Minnie balls rained down. Suddenly, something struck the old house. Wood splintered and stone shattered. Part of the floor fell into the cellar raining dust and dirt all over me. I was not hurt, but I did not try to leave the ruins of this house.

I closed my eyes and remembered good old Elijah who remained in the cave during the tempest, the earthquake, and the fire. Only when he had heard the still small voice of the Lord did he venture out. I waited and waited for the still small voice. I know that the Lord is my sure refuge and could protect me in this crumbling house in the midst of a battlefield as well as any parlor in a city. The small still voice of the Lord coincided with the stilling of the muskets and the quieting of the cannons. The Rebels fell back and took a new position. Assured this was the right time, I escaped quickly over into Federal lines.

I raced to headquarters and reported the facts I had overheard. I pulled out the documents and handed them to General Heintzelman. Imagine my surprise to learn these were orders for the Confederate commanders with instructions for how and when to move to capture Washington.

But they will not capture Washington now—will they!

Your determined Yankee friend and soldier,

Baltimore, Maryland

August 26, 1862

Dear Emma,

It's been two days now, and I still cannot figure out the rhyme. I know I should be at the bakery at noon on a Monday, Tuesday, or Wednesday. But I don't know whom I am to meet. I've gone over it again and again in my mind:

Adam was first, then came Eve
R-S or was it T-U-V?

Is it a man named Adam? A woman named Eve? And how will I know the last name? Should I try to unscramble the letters RSTUV? Is it a person by the name of Vurts? Struv?

Today is Tuesday. I must go to the bakery tomorrow or else I lose my chance until next week. Great-Auntie is trying to secure passage for all three of us on the flag-of-truce boat. She is sending messages to Washington and to Great-Uncle Chester. Once we are cleared to go, I will have to leave.

I simply must get this message to the right person. Perhaps if I go down tomorrow to the bakery and wait, I will learn something, anything, that can help me solve this mystery.

Tonight Great-Auntie is taking us to a concert. Sissy bemoans not having a nicer dress, but I told her she could wear my hat tonight and she was quite pleased.

Great-Auntie and I have had many conversations. But with Sissy near, I haven't told her anything about my missions. Once or twice she has had a moment to tell me how proud she is of you. She says Great-Uncle Chester admires your commitment to your duties. He hears great things about you from some of his surgeon friends who are in the field.

Your friend,

Mollie

Baltimore, Maryland

August 27, 1862

Dear Emma,

I asked Great-Auntie if I could go to the bakery again, and she granted me permission. It is only a two-block walk from her home. Sissy wanted to find where Hetty Cary lived before she fled to Richmond so she left about the same time. She did not seem suspicious at all of my asking to go alone to the bakery.

I arrived there at eleven o'clock. I took my time selecting a biscuit. I buttered it slowly and sat at a little table in the corner. That spot allowed me to be near the window and the entrance and directly under the clock.

The bakery filled with customers, some of whom seemed like regulars. The baker greeted many of them by name. I wish he were the man to take my message.

The clock chimed each quarter hour. I pretended to read my book—*The History of Baltimore*. At forty-five minutes after eleven, the clock chimed again and a Federal soldier, a captain, came in the store. He talked in low tones with the baker. Could he be the one? Yet, he left with his bread and hardly glanced in my direction.

I was so tense! I could hear the massive hands of the clock as they moved the space of each minute. Very quickly, it was noon. Bong. Bong. Bong. Yet no person—man or woman—Adam or Eve—appeared. Bong. Bong. Bong. Even the baker left the counter to tend his ovens. Bong. Bong. Bong. My book burned in my hands as I thought about the message inside it that I needed to get to the right person. Bong. Bong. Bong. Twelve strikes.

The door opened and a young man who looked about eighteen or nineteen years of age came into the store. He didn't even look my way. "Hmmm . . . hmmm. Smells awfully good in here!" he said to no one in particular. "I just love pie days. Mondays, Tuesdays, and Wednesdays. The best days in the week."

He gazed into the cases trying to make his selection. After a few minutes, he turned in my direction, smiled and said, "It's the rest of the week without any pies that makes you want to cry."

I gave a start. Why, he was almost quoting the rhyme! Could this be him—the person to whom I was to give the message? I had to be sure. I pretended to read but watched him out of the corner of my eye. The baker came to the counter and said, "Young Mr. Evers, what can I get you today?"

The young man smiled broadly and said, "Two cookies, sir." When he made his purchase, he walked over to my table, laid one of the cookies down on the table on a cloth napkin, and then, he left the store.

I stared at the cookie. Was it a clue? Was there something written on the napkin? I turned the napkin over but found no writing in code or otherwise. Disappointed, at the next chime of the clock, I got up to leave.

As I walked home, I replayed the scene over and over again in my mind. Then it hit me. Mr. E ver-s. The baker had called him Mr. Evers. E-V-E-R-S. EVE R-S. EVERS! It was him. I ran back to the bakery as fast as I could. I looked all around the bakery and inside, but Mr. Evers had vanished. I walked home dejected. I had completely missed it. All the clues, right there in front of me, and I couldn't put them together quickly enough.

Now it was too late. It was Wednesday and there would be no more chance of meeting him until next Monday. Emma, what if this message is urgent? What if Great-Auntie gets us a flag-of-truce boat before next Monday?

Oh, Emma, this spy business is not so easy after all.

Your discouraged friend,

Mollie

Baltimore, Maryland

August 29, 1862

Dear Emma,

I simply had to put it out of my mind. I cannot return until Monday, and it looks like Great-Auntie's arrangements for us to travel by a flag-of-truce boat have hit some problems. At least we won't leave before next Monday.

Great-Auntie, Sissy, and I have had such fun. I've almost forgotten what fun is like. We went to the theater and a concert and Great-Auntie introduced us to her new friends. They are surprised when we tell them what Richmond is like now. Before the war, people traveled freely between Baltimore and Richmond. Now, most of their news about Richmond comes from the newspapers.

The best time we had with Great-Auntie was when we told her about Daddy's letters. I noticed Sissy did not share what was in hers, and I certainly did not share what was in mine. There would be time for that later when I could tell Great-Auntie the whole story and how Daddy's letter affected my decisions about certain things related to this great war.

Sissy and I have worked so hard for so many months for the effort—sewing uniforms, rolling bandages, nursing the wounded, and caring for boarders. We thoroughly enjoyed being taken care of by Great-Auntie. I think she enjoyed it too for she pampered us exquisitely. I just wish Momma could have been here to enjoy a rest from her labors.

Tomorrow, Great-Auntie is holding a reception in our honor. She has invited a number of young ladies and young men to make our acquaintance. It's too late for Sissy, but Great-Auntie still holds out hope that I'll marry a Northerner. She told me she has invited several young medical students from Johns Hopkins to attend.

"Younger versions of Great-Uncle Chester?" I inquired sweetly.

"You could do worse," she responded smiling.

Of course, that was all Sissy needed to inspire another shopping trip. She had carefully counted out the gold she had remaining after paying for Lem's uniform and shirts. With some additional funds provided by Great-Auntie, we three were off again shopping for new dresses. I almost felt guilty, as I knew these funds could be spent on medicine and food, but Great-Auntie insisted both of us have a new dress for the party. "Even if we cannot smuggle them back," Great-Auntie insisted, "I shall keep them here for you until the end of the war." It was frivolous, extravagant, and oh so appreciated!

Sissy and I had the time of our lives trying on the latest fashions. We finally made our selections and Great-Auntie paid to have them delivered to her home. We then went to tea at the hotel around the corner from the bakery.

The lobby was filled with Federal soldiers, many of whom were officers. Great-Auntie conversed easily with the ones she knew. They asked about Great-Uncle Chester to which she always replied, "Mending you boys as fast as he can!" Sissy was uncomfortable, and I know she felt she was disloyal to the Confederacy sitting in the hotel populated with Federal officers and sipping delicious tea—with sugar. I squeezed her hand under the table so that she would know I understood.

I'm the one who is disloyal to the Confederacy. I'm the one who takes the messages from one Federal agent to another. Yet, in my heart, I know it is the right thing to do. We must preserve the Union and that Union must be free of slavery. I know what I am doing is just a small thing but like you, Emma, I have to make a difference.

I count the minutes until Monday at noon.

Your friend,

Mollie

Baltimore, Maryland

August 30, 1862

Dear Emma,

It is very late, but I must stay up to write you. Tonight, Great-Auntie held the reception here at her home for Sissy and me. She introduced us to many wonderful young people. It took me back to a time several years ago when there was a similar reception for Sissy and me at our cousins in Connecticut—a time when I met a young man named Franklin Thompson, a Bible salesman. Ah! But he was not what he seemed. He was a she.

I thank God for the friendship that developed between us. You trusted me with your secret then and now. Your letters show me how God has used you in many ways to help wounded and dying men know of his gift of grace and salvation. There will be many who will greet you one day in heaven standing next to your Savior cheering when they hear him say, "Well done, good and faithful servant. Well done, Emma Edmonds."

You inspire me, Emma—you, and the Greats, and yes, Daddy. You have all inspired me to take risks when it is necessary to accomplish a great goal. Each of you in your own way has made me think about this war inside out and upside down.

It is very complicated, and I don't pretend to understand it all, but this one thing I know. Very committed, caring people on both sides of this war believe they are right and believe God will vindicate their position. But how can the South win if it stands for slavery? How much longer can God permit our country to enslave those he created, and call them *our property!* I do pray this war is over soon and that the entire country will agree on this question of slavery.

At the reception tonight, like so much in this war, music and dancing and laughter and fun were ours to enjoy until we heard the news. At the second Battle of Bull Run, the Federals were barely holding their lines just miles from Washington. Everyone fell silent at the party. Everyone knows that if Washington is captured, Baltimore is not far away. And, if Washington falls to the Confederates, then the great experiment of the United States is over.

Sissy should have been glad for the Confederate victory, but she whispered to me in a plaintive voice, "Lem . . . I have to know if he is safe."

Great-Auntie stopped the music and asked us to all join with her in a prayer for the men and boys in the field. I know she was thinking of her husband and whether he was on duty on the battlefield. Sissy was thinking of Lem and whether or not he was wounded, and I, of course, as always, silently but prayerfully, thought about you, my dear disguised soldier in blue.

May God be with you, Emma.

Your friend,

Mollie

Richmond, Virginia

August 31, 1862

Dear Emma,

We have heard there was more fighting today. I continue to pray moment by moment for your safety and protection. Great-Auntie, Sissy, and I attended church today—a day set aside to reflect on the sins of our nation.

I've been thinking about the days of prayer and fasting that each side has proclaimed throughout the war. I do not think a day of praying to win is what turns the heart of God. No, I am quite convinced that what will turn his heart to us is when we turn our hearts to him and confess our sin. Then he can hear us. Then he can turn to us. Then, and only then, can he heal our land.

Today, that is the fast I undertake.

Your friend,

Mollie

Baltimore, Maryland

September 1, 1862

Dear Emma,

It is Monday. Today is the day. Noon at the bakery—nothing shall keep me from my appointment with young Mr. Evers.

Emma, I wrote that this morning, but I had no idea I would not be able to finish this letter until late at night. At eleven o'clock today, as I prepared to leave for the bakery, a Federal officer appeared at our doorstep. Great-Auntie nearly fainted for she was afraid it was bad news about Great-Uncle Chester. The young officer assured her he was there to provide details on the passage on the flag-of-truce boat that was leaving first thing in the morning from the harbor.

He told us what we would be permitted to bring and that our persons and our belongings would be searched. He leveled his eyes at Sissy and me and added, "Anyone found with contraband will be summarily removed from the boat." Sissy held her breath and her face was calm. Only the twisting of a strand of hair gave her away. Yet, she quickly stopped the twisting and stood up straight. I could see the fire in her eyes and the determination in her spirit. She did not come this far for Lem's uniform to leave without it!

Great-Auntie said I had no time for the bakery, and that sweets on a flag-of-truce boat would be confiscated anyway because they are contraband foods. She then directed Sissy and me to tend to a long list of things we had to do to be ready by seven in the morning. My list had nothing to do with going down to Charles Street, and it was already 11:45. If we left in the morning, all would be lost. I would return to Richmond with my message as surely as I had left with it.

Suddenly, Sissy said, "Great-Auntie! We have to pick up your purse, the one with the needles and threads and gold lace for Lem's uniform. The tailor delivered the shawls and our gray petticoats but he forgot to send the purse."

I jumped at the opportunity. "I'll go—quick as lightning. Why, I'll be back before the clock strikes one." Great-Auntie agreed, and I headed down to Charles Street. The tailor was just a block away from the bakery. I carried my book under my arm, which thankfully, Great-Auntie and Sissy were too distracted to notice.

I nearly ran the entire way and arrived at the store just as the clock began to strike noon. No Mr. Evers. My eyes darted to each customer. He had to come. He just had to. Twelve bongs sounded and no Mr. Evers. I shifted my weight from one foot to the other. I tried to calm myself down, but fifteen more minutes passed with no sign of Mr. Evers. My heart raced as I watched the clock tick by fifteen more minutes. As the clock struck the half hour, I could not wait any longer. I stood to leave just as Mr. Evers jauntily strode inside the store. He tipped his hat to me, and said, "No cookie, today?"

I had to find out if he was the one. "I much prefer pickled peaches," I replied.

He laughed. "To cookies? During the war, when sweets are a treat? I would think a young Southern girl like you would want a cookie a day!"

How did he know I was Southern? I suppose it could have been my Virginia accent. Or perhaps he had some information from Miss Van Lew about me? He purchased two cookies and said, "Would you care to share one with me?"

I didn't have much time. I had to get to the tailor's shop and home before one o'clock. I impatiently nibbled at my cookie, wanting desperately for him to reveal himself to me. I thought and thought and then tried one more tactic. "I do not even know your proper name—to thank you—for the cookie, of course."

"Mr. Evers. Adam Evers. Formerly of Richmond. Now studying medicine in Baltimore. At your service, Miss . . ."

"Miss Turner. Mollie Turner. Still of Richmond. Visiting Baltimore."

"Ah, I see you have a book about Baltimore? Could I see it?"

I clutched the book to my chest. Then I realized he was *Adam* Evers. Adam Eve RS. He could be the one, but I had to know for sure. I handed him the book and watched him steadily.

"Hmm . . . *The History of Baltimore*." He looked inside and read a few sentences. Then he turned the book and stared at the spine. He turned the book to me with the spine facing me, tapped the spine, and said, "I imagine that this book is filled with secrets about this old city."

Was he trying to tell me something?

"Secrets that would take quite a historian to decipher," he continued.

It must be him!

"I fancy myself a historian. I would love to read this book. Might I borrow it?"

I stared steadily at him. It all fit. His name was Adam Evers. He appeared at the bakery on Mondays, Tuesdays, and Wednesdays at noon. And he seemed to know there might be a secret message in the spine of the book.

"And how, pray tell, would you return it to me? There's been no mail between North and South for more than a year."

"Why, Miss Mollie, I would commandeer the flag-of-truce boat and take it to you myself!"

We both laughed at such an idea.

"Then," I asked, "how would you find me when you got to Richmond?"

"Well, first I would stop by Jeff Davis' home and inquire where the most beautiful girl in Richmond lived. But if he could not tell me, I would go to a delightful shop on Main Street and inquire about the young lady who always purchases pickled peaches and returns only the pits."

I gave a start. He knew about Mr. and Mrs. Simpson and their shop on Main Street. He knew about the peach pit sign, though he did not wear one now.

"Then you must read this book," I exclaimed. "By all means, read it cover to cover. Let nothing escape your

attention. Then and only then will you know what I know."
Assured that my mission was successful, I rose from the table.
Adam Evers rose and opened the door for me. After a few
steps, I turned to wave good-bye but he had already picked
up the book and slipped out the door. The handsome and
mysterious young Mr. Evers was gone from my life.

I hurried to the tailor's shop and picked up the purse.
First, the tailor showed me the very fine work he had done in
the lining. I felt all around the bottom, but could find no
evidence of the needle or thread or gold lace. I thanked him
and quickly returned home with both missions accomplished.

The rest of the day, Great-Auntie barked orders at Sissy
and me. I don't think you or Lem have a tougher drill sergeant
than the one we had today. She made sure we had our outfits,
our trunks, and our stories all shipshape before bed.

Great-Auntie is firmly in charge of our venture home,
and told us to follow her lead tomorrow. Frankly, with all that
Sissy and I have been through the last few weeks, we were
happy to follow whatever orders she gave. We packed our
trunks carefully. It would not do for Great-Auntie to be
accused of assisting Confederate girls to smuggle contraband
goods through the lines, especially when she had used Great-
Uncle Chester's rank and reputation to secure the passes for
us from the War Department.

Sissy looked at her new dress longingly and then packed
it away in a drawer at Great-Auntie's home. I stared at my hat
a very long time. I thought and thought and thought about
how to get it back with me. We were already heavy laden with

our petticoats that concealed the Confederate gray cloth and buttons for Lem's uniform, and our new shawls made out of flannel for Lem's shirts. Great-Auntie insisted that I leave it, and with great sadness I bid the lovely hat adieu.

I had not told Great-Auntie, but I had added some tea and coffee in the false bottom of my trunk. I wanted something for Momma, and she does so love her coffee. If only I could have hidden some sugar to go with it. I checked again to make sure the false bottom was secure and thought that Momma should have a reward for her troubles. I also included extra needles, pins, buttons, and threads for Momma. She sacrificed so much. I must get these things through for her. They all fit nicely under the false bottom of the trunk.

Sissy fell asleep early. Great-Auntie, all tuckered out from her day of bellowing orders, slowly sipped her cup of tea with sugar, a Federal luxury she would soon be without. "Child, if only Chester could see you now. Soon the boys will come courting. That is, of course, once they come home from the war. I wonder whom you will marry, dear. It will have to be someone full of adventure—someone with integrity and spirit. Someone like your great-uncle, I do imagine."

"I miss him so much, Great-Auntie. When will we be able to see him again?"

"I think that is the question of the long war. When, oh when, will it be over? It is every mother's and every wife's cry. This is such a difficult, difficult war, and it has taken a great toll on all the families. I'm glad your father did not have to see our nation torn up like this. Now, tell me more about your letter from your daddy," she said as she patted me on the arm.

I snuggled up close to her on the sofa and said, "Great-Auntie, there is so much I have to tell you." And then, I told her everything. I told her how I had struggled with my thoughts about the war. I told her about Miss Van Lew, the books I had read, and Constance and her views on slavery even though she was a Virginian. I told her about nursing the wounded at Robertson Hospital; and then I told her about my missions, including the one that ended today. She sat quietly listening to my stories, asking a question every now and then. Mostly, she just listened. Then when I was done, she squeezed me tight, and with tears in her eyes, said, "Chester is right, Mollie, dear, you do have a very good head on those pretty shoulders."

Your friend,

Mollie

Manassas, Virginia

September 3, 1862

Dear Mollie,

We met the enemy again in the Second Battle of Bull Run. Oh yes, I am sure you Confederates will call it the Second Battle of Manassas. This time we were stronger and more experienced, and we were ready. But, Mollie, we were soundly trounced.

During the fighting, the commanding generals ordered me behind Rebel lines four times over a ten-day span. I moved back and forth along the lines observing the troops and their artillery and then reporting to headquarters. As always, I managed to escape unobserved by friend or foe. The last, during the Battle of Chantilly, was the worst.

The night of the battle, as I edged my way back to the Federal lines, a soldier rode up to the picket line. I thought he was a Rebel officer until the Rebel pickets fired at him. The soldier fell from his force, and the pickets ran to learn who their victim was. When they realized they had killed a Federal general, they shouted for joy. But when I heard it was General Kearney, I fell to my knees.

Mollie, I would willingly have died in his place to save such a great general in the Union army. Sometimes I don't understand God's ways. Why was he taken while I, poor insignificant creature, was left? I have a heart and soul as fully devoted to the Union cause as Kearney's was, but I certainly lack the ability to accomplish the same results.

While the attention of the pickets was drawn in another direction, I lost no time in my escape. I reported to head-quarters, where Colonel Poe ordered me to take certain dispatches and documents to General McClelland. I rode as fast as I could to Washington. General Lee comes closer to Washington. I have even heard there is a warship anchored in the Potomac to take away President Lincoln and his cabinet members if the capital should fall to General Lee.

Discouraging times, Mollie. Very, very discouraging times.

Your friend,

G.

Richmond, Virginia

September 10, 1862

Dear Emma,

When we first arrived to board the flag-of-truce boat, the Federal officers locked us in our staterooms. They searched all baggage and three hours later, two guards took Sissy and me to be searched. The woman who conducted our search seemed bored with the task and barely bothered searching our clothes. I prayed silently that the inspectors would be as disinterested when searching my baggage. I sighed wistfully thinking about my hat left in Great-Auntie's house. They even had us undo our hair and searched it for contraband.

The guards marched us back to our stateroom. Assuming it was her turn now, Great-Auntie rose. One guard said, "Madam, as the eldest of our passengers and by courtesy of the captain, you are excused from the search."

Great-Auntie thanked him profusely. When he left, she said, "That was close."

Sissy said, "But Great-Auntie, we made sure you carried no contraband. Why were you worried?"

Great-Auntie fished around under her billowing skirts, held something up high and said, "This!" I clapped my hands.

Great Auntie proudly held out my hat. We threw our arms around her and danced in the stateroom.

The rest of the trip was horrible. Mothers who risked everything and spent their last dollar on shoes for their children watched as soldiers confiscated the shoes. Soldiers stripped the necessities for life from women who were just trying to help their families survive. Needles, pins, thread, cloth, sugar, coffee, tea, lemons, and limes were all taken.

The Federals gave us each a cup of dirty water in a tin cup to drink, a chunk of ham, and bread for our meals. That night we slept on filthy mattresses with no sheets. We silently thanked the tailor for his flannel shawls that hid cloth for Confederate shirts and now served as our blankets.

Never were we so glad to be home. Momma welcomed us with hot food, warm baths, and clean beds. We enjoyed it all, but not before we gave her a salute for successfully fooling the Federals with her false-bottom trunk. We presented her with needles and thread and coffee and tea, and showed her how the tailor had hidden Lem's uniform in pieces right under the noses of the searchers. But it was my hat that got the most attention. And of course, the story of how Great-Auntie Belle helped smuggle contraband goods to the Confederacy!

We've been busy here nursing the many wounded from the Battle at Manassas. Even Great-Auntie helps. Watching her nurse the Confederate soldiers with as much energy as if they were Federals, I love her even more. It's the women who really understand the toll this war has taken on our country.

Your friend,

Mollie

Sharpsburg, Maryland

September 21, 1862

Dear Mollie,

The morning of September 17th, the sound of the crack of muskets and the boom of cannons signaled that the fighting had begun. During this time, the doctors and nurses stood by. All we could do was wait for the first to fall and then rush to tend them. Mollie, waiting for the wounded to fall is the worst part of my duties.

Not even what I saw at Fair Oaks compares to what I saw on the bloody battlefields of Antietam. So many men and boys died. We worked hard all day to take the wounded from the field on stretchers so that the doctors could try to save their lives. The surgeons worked without stopping at great risk to themselves. Several surgeons were killed that day.

Our nearest hospital was within range of enemy shells. We had five other camp hospitals nearby. We carried stretcher after stretcher of wounded men to waiting ambulances. Here generals and privates lay side by side, as death is no respecter of rank. I washed their wounds and gave them water to drink, while they waited for the surgeons.

Over and over again, dying men lifted their voices in agony. When I could, I would ask each man if he knew the Savior, and while I gave him water from a canteen, I prayed over him and shared a Bible verse or two. The idea that any of these young men could die this day without knowing Jesus as their Redeemer spurred me on.

In this way, I spent the day and the evening. That night, I passed by a pale, sweet face of a young soldier who was severely wounded. The boy grew faint from the loss of blood. I stooped down and asked if there was anything I could do for him. The soldier looked at me with clear, intelligent eyes, said, "Yes, yes. There is something to be done, and quickly for I am dying."

I left the boy and quickly ran to one of the surgeons. He came back with me, examined him, and agreed that this soldier would not live to see the sun rise. I gave the boy some water from my canteen. The boy motioned me closer with a trembling hand. I knelt down beside him and listened with breathless attention to catch the words that fell from his dying lips.

"I am not what I seem. I am a female. I enlisted from the purest motives and have remained undiscovered and unsuspected. I have no mother or father. My only brother was killed today. I closed his eyes an hour before I was wounded. I shall soon be with him for I am a Christian. My trust is in God and I will die in peace, but I wish you to bury me with your own hands that none may know after my death that I am a girl. I know I can trust you."

I spoke gently to her. "Yes, I will do what you ask." I found a chaplain, and we prayed with her. I stayed with her until she died about an hour later, and then I did as she asked. I found a spot under a mulberry tree where in another time, the sounds of birds, not cannons, will be heard. Her sorrows are now over and her race is won. She's found the heavenly shore and touched the face of God.

Mollie, this girl's death affected me more than any other death I have witnessed in this war. As I knelt by her grave, tucked under a tree on a hill overlooking a field where so many died, tears poured down my face. I cried for her. I cried for this country. I cried for myself. This girl could just as easily have been me. I don't know why God has spared my life so far, but may I serve him with all my heart and soul just as this young girl did.

Your friend,

Richmond, Virginia

September 24, 1862

Dear Emma,

Your good letter from Sharpsburg arrived today. I don't know how it came through Federal lines to me so fast. Perhaps it was carried on the wings of angels.

I welcomed the news of your safety with joy. I welcome the strength of our friendship with a thankful heart. I noticed you signed your name Emma this time. I am glad, for you *are* Emma. Don't let all the days in the blue uniform cause you to forget the sweet, sensitive, and beautiful girl that you are.

Your letter reveals your weary soul. You have faithfully tended the wounded and dying for so long and carried out all of your duties with courage and grace. You move from person to person, duty to duty, in the midst of danger without any thought of your own safety. Your faith in God has not wavered amidst the horrors of what man can do to man. You have trusted him each day with your life and led so many others to know his love.

You have longed for all to know freedom. For the slave, you have desired freedom of body, mind, and spirit—no longer in bondage to any man. For everyone you meet, you have desired freedom of salvation that comes from Jesus Christ alone. You have labored well. You have labored long. Now you must rest, dear Emma—rest in the knowledge that all is not in vain.

Charlie just came by with word that two days ago, President Lincoln announced his Emancipation Proclamation. In just a few months, on the first of January, all slaves everywhere will be free. Now we must continue to fight your way and mine—to make sure that it is the Union that prevails. Then we shall have a glorious reunion. Then we must tell the Greats all that has happened!

You, dear Emma, are a remarkable lady. There will come a day when you lay down the blue uniform and willingly take up your skirts again. When that day comes, I will contribute to your outfit its crowning glory. You, my friend, shall have my contraband hat!

Your friend forever,

Mollie

Liberty Letters

Now the Lord is Spirit; and where the Spirit of the Lord is, there is Liberty.

2 Corinthians 3:17

Dear Reader,

When I wrote Liberty Letters, I intended to communicate America's journey of freedom and also to illustrate the personal faith journey of girls who made bold choices to help others and in doing so, helped shape the course of history. Through their stories, we learn the facts, customs, lifestyles of days gone by, and so much more.

The girls I wrote about didn't consider themselves part of "history." Few people do. These were ordinary girls going about their lives when challenging times occurred in the communities in which they lived. They discovered integrity, courage, hope, and faith within themselves as they met these challenges with creativity and innovation. American history is steeped with just these kinds of people. These people embody liberty.

At least 400, and maybe as many as 1,000, disguised women were soldiers in the Civil War. Emma Edmonds, a private in the Union Army, was one of those women. Not only do military records confirm her service, but she left us with her own story, Nurse and Spy in the Union Army, first published in 1864. No one suspected she wrote about herself at the time, however, because the idea that a woman could serve in the military was pure fiction!

Yet twenty years later, Emma's military pension file, the Congressional record, sworn affidavits of fellow soldiers and officers, and Emma's official statement, provided the proof that the United States government needed to declare that Emma Edmonds Seelye and Private Franklin Thompson of Company F of the 2nd Michigan Infantry were one and the same.

I wanted to tell Emma's story and explore the motivation behind her commitment. After all, Emma could have served as a civilian nurse—as she did with the Christian Commission in West Virginia when she reclaimed her female identity. To tell Emma's story, I adapted some of Emma's adventures in Nurse and Spy. I often kept her words as close to her own voice as possible, especially where she shared her personal Christian faith and beliefs.

Did Emma have a friend like Mollie during the war? As far as we know, Emma kept her identity a closely guarded secret. With the exception of one fellow soldier, it is likely that no one knew her secret at the time. But as an author, I wondered what it would have been like if Emma had shared her secret—and her adventures—with a good friend like Mollie Turner. That part of the story is fiction. Yet, one can imagine the need Emma had to share her real self with someone. Perhaps that is why she so quickly wrote her story after leaving the army—she just had to tell someone about her adventures, even if no one knew it was she who had them!

Your Friend,

Nancy LeSourd

Epilogue

By the time of the Emancipation Proclamation, the war was not even half over. More hardship, grief, and loss would come to both the North and the South. This "great war" often required people on both sides of the many issues that divided our country to decide for themselves what they believed and what they would be willing to sacrifice for those beliefs.

Emma Edmonds a.k.a. Private Franklin Thompson

There is much more to Emma Edmonds' story than could be told here. When Emma became ill with malaria, the doctors required who they thought was Private Franklin Thompson to be hospitalized. Emma had a tough decision to make—hope she would not be examined and her secret discovered or desert the army? In the spring of 1863, Private Frank Thompson disappeared from the ranks of Company F of the 2nd Michigan Volunteer Infantry.

While recovering from her illness, Frank became Emma once again. During this time she wrote *Nurse and Spy in the Union Army*. Not yet ready to reveal the connection between herself and Frank Thompson, she used initials and changed some details to obscure the identities of the main characters. Mr. Hurlburt, her previous employer, published *Nurse and Spy*, which Emma dedicated to the sick and wounded soldiers of the Army of the Potomac. It was an overnight best seller. Emma donated the proceeds from the book to the Christian Commission and to veterans' aid organizations.

In 1864, with the Civil War still raging and many wounded soldiers still in need of care, Emma joined the Christian Commission and worked at a hospital in Harper's Ferry, West Virginia. In 1867 she married Linus Seelye, and together they raised a family, finally settling in Texas.

Fifteen years later, Emma contacted soldiers who had served with her, and surprised them with the true story of "Frank Thompson." Emma sought their assistance to secure a government pension for her years of military service. Her fellow soldiers submitted numerous affidavits to Congress that attested to her faithful service as soldier and nurse in the Union army. The many affirmations may best be summed up by the captain who mustered her into the army:

"S. Emma E. Seelye, by her uniform faithfulness, bravery, and efficiency, and by her pure morals and Christian character, won the respect, admiration, and confidence of both officers and men in said company and regiment." – Captain William Morse

In 1884 the U.S. Congress granted Emma her soldier's pension, stating that the fact that "Franklin Thompson and Mrs. Sarah E. E. Seelye are one and the same person is established by abundance of proof and beyond a doubt." In 1897 Emma became the only woman to be mustered into the Grand Army of the Republic as a regular member, and in 1988 she was inducted into the Military Intelligence Hall of Fame.

Much of Emma's story as told in the history books focuses on her bravery as a soldier and spy or her acts of compassion as a field nurse. Rarely do they mention her motivation for her service—her Christian faith. However, her own story in *Nurse and Spy* reveals the depth of her faith commitment, and the final statement in her book expresses the passion of her heart:

And now I lay aside my pen, hoping that after "this cruel war is over" and peace shall have once more shed her sweet influence over our land, I may be permitted to resume it again to record the annihilation of rebellion, and the final triumph of Truth, Right and Liberty.

O Lord of Peace, who art Lord of righteousness,
Constrain the anguished worlds from sin and grief
Pierce them with conscience, purge them with redress,
And give us peace which is no counterfeit!

Elizabeth Van Lew

Elizabeth Van Lew developed her own, carefully guarded code and sent important information to Union generals through trusted individuals. Ordinary people such as store clerks, shoemakers, and servants formed her secret network.

False bottom trays, hollowed-out soles of shoes, and books hid secrets for Van Lew's network. Miss Van Lew avoided detection throughout the entire war. After the war, General Ulysses S. Grant said, "You have sent me the most valuable information received from Richmond during the war." When he became president of the United States, he appointed her postmaster of Richmond, a position she held for his two terms as president.

However, many in Richmond regarded Miss Van Lew as a traitor to the Southern cause. She lived a very lonely life and died nearly penniless in 1900. Relatives of some of the former Libby prisoners she had helped, including descendants of Paul Revere, raised money for her headstone. On the stone, they inscribed these words:

She risked everything that is dear to man—
friends, fortune, comfort, health, life itself,
all for one absorbing desire of her heart—
that slavery might be abolished and the Union preserved.

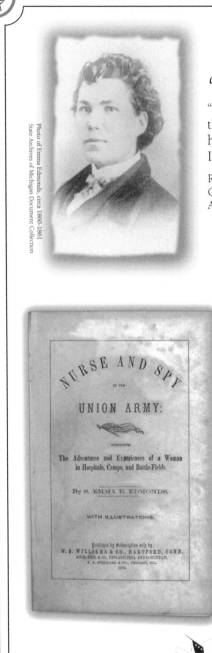

Emma Edmonds
circa 1860-1861, in male civilian dress

" . . . I had no other motive in enlisting than love to God and love for suffering humanity. I felt called to go and do what I could for the defense of the right. . . . "

Report 820 to accompany H.R. 5334, United States Congress, March 18, 1884, Franklin Thompson, Alias, S.E.E. Seelye, Statement of S. Emma E. Seelye

Union Soldier's Canteen, circa 1861-65

NURSE AND SPY

IN THE

UNION ARMY:

COMPRISING

The Adventures and Experiences of a Woman
in Hospitals, Camps, and Battle-Fields.

By S. EMMA E. EDMONDS.

WITH ILLUSTRATIONS.

Published by Subscription only by
W. S. WILLIAMS & CO., HARTFORD, CONN.
JONES BROS. & CO., PHILADELPHIA AND CINCINNATI.
A. A. STODDARD & CO., CHICAGO, ILL.
1865.

Copy of *Nurse and Spy in the Union Army: The Adventures and Experiences of a Woman in Hospitals, Camps, and Battle Fields* by S. Emma E. Edmonds, 1864

Post Office at Headquarters,
Army of the Potomac

Receiving letters from home was an important part of the soldier's life, whether he fought for the Union or the Confederacy.

Cross Carved by Unknown Soldier of the 77th NY Vol. Infantry

Wounded Soldiers in Hospital, Circa 1861-1865

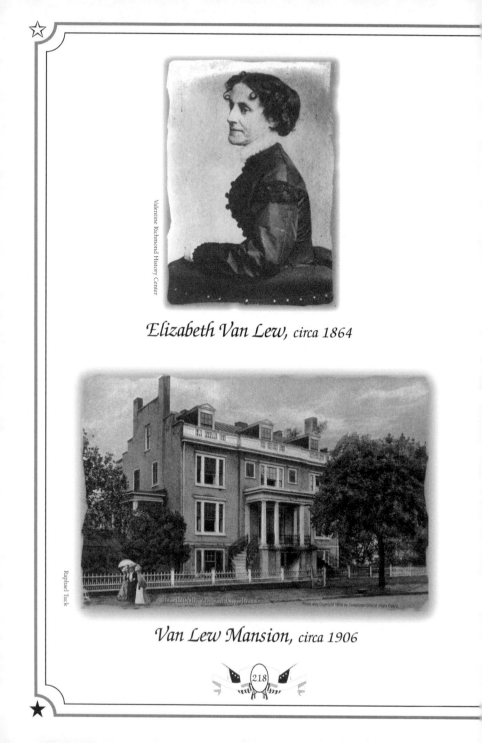

Elizabeth Van Lew, circa 1864

Van Lew Mansion, circa 1906

Elizabeth Van Lew's Cipher Code

Van Lew relied on a cipher code, hidden in her watch case, and a colorless liquid to create her dispatches to Union generals. The code appeared when milk was applied to the message.

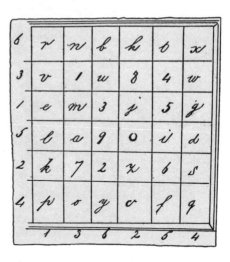

"LIBBY PRISON."
THE ONLY PICTURE IN EXISTENCE.
AS IT APPEARED
AUGUST 23, 1863.

Libby Prison, 1863

Sally Tompkins

Sally Tompkins nursed 1,333 Confederate soldiers in her 22 bed Robertson Hospital in Richmond with the remarkable record of only 73 deaths over a four year period. Captain Sally sent off her recovered patient with a knapsack packed with a blanket, clean clothes, warm socks she often knitted herself, and a copy of the Gospels bound in oil cloth.

In the Hospital,
1861

☆

by
William Ludwell Sheppard

One soldier's unraveled tent became another soldier's knitted socks at the hands of Mary Greenhow Lee, sister-in-law of Confederate spy Rose Greenhow.

UNITED STATES CHRISTIAN COMMISSION

U. S. CHRISTIAN COMMISSION

Negative by J. Gardner   Positive by A. Gardner
HEADQUARTERS CHRISTIAN COMMISSION, IN THE FIELD, GERMANTOWN, SEPTEMBER, 1863   PLATE 53

Christian Commission in the Field

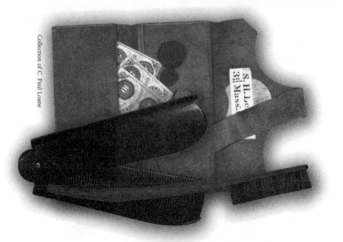

Property of Pvt. Stephen H. Leonard, Company A, 3rd Company, Massachusetts Volunteer Calvary, sent to his parents after his death in action in 1864. Among other items, his property included a wallet, toothbrush, patriotic bookmark, a diary, comb, and button bag.